Maybe she should walk away now.

Even as the thought came to her, she knew she wouldn't do it. Partly because she wasn't sure her knees would hold and partly because there was nowhere she'd rather be than right there, smiling up at this charming, beautiful man—and having him smile back at her.

"I'm Nic, by the way," he said.

"I'm Desi."

"Would you like to dance, Desi?" he asked, taking the champagne glass from her hand and depositing it on a passing tray.

She should say no. She had a million things to do here tonight, and not one of them involved getting swept onto the dance floor by some hot, rich guy who had probably forgotten more about seduction than she'd ever known. But even as the thought occurred to her, even knowing that she might very well get burned before the night was over, she nodded.

He held her closer than was necessary for a first dance between strangers. One hand on her lower back, his fingers curving over the soft swell of her hip. His hard, strong chest brushing against hers with each step.

Desi felt herself melting. Felt herself falling a little more under his spell. She knew it was stupid, ridiculous, *insane*, but for the first time in her life, she didn't care.

Tightening her hand where it rested against the back of his neck, she pulled him forward, pulled him down, down, down, until his lips met hers.

Pursued

TRACY WOLFF

First published in Great Britain 2015
by Mills & Boon, an imprint of Harlequin (UK) Limited,
Large Print edition 2015
Eton House, 18-24 Paradise Road,
Richmond, Surrey, TW9 1SR

© 2015 Tracy L. Deebs-Elkenaney

ISBN: 978-0-263-26046-5

Tracy Wolff collects books, English degrees and lipsticks, and has been known to forget where—and sometimes who—she is when immersed in a great novel. At six, she wrote her first short story—something with a rainbow and a prince—and at seven, she ventured into the wonderful world of girls' lit with her first Judy Blume novel. By ten, she'd read everything in the young-adult and classics sections of her local bookstore, so in desperation her mom started her on romance novels. And from the first page of the first book, Tracy knew she'd found her lifelong love. Tracy lives in Texas with her husband and three sons, where she pens romance novels and teaches writing at her local community college.

One

He was the most beautiful man she'd ever seen.

Desi Maddox knew that sounded excessive, melodramatic even, considering she was standing in a room filled with beautiful people in even more beautiful clothes, but the longer she stood there staring at him, the more convinced she became. He. Was. Gorgeous. So gorgeous that for long seconds he blinded her to everything around her, even the glitter of gems and flash of high society that under normal circumstances would be impossible to ignore.

But these were far from normal circumstances. How could they be when his emerald gaze met hers over the sea of people stretching between them and her knees trembled. Actually trembled. Up until now, she'd always thought that was a cliché best saved for chick flicks and romance novels. But here she was in the middle of a crowded ballroom and all she could do was stand there as her heart raced, her palms grew damp and her knees actually trembled with the force of her reaction to a man she'd never seen before and more than likely would never see again.

Which was probably a good thing, and knowing she wouldn't see him again was exactly what she needed to remind herself why she was here among the best and brightest of San Diego's high society. Scoping out hot men was definitely not what her boss was paying her for.

More's the pity.

Shaking her head in an effort to clear it, Desi forced herself to glance away from his mesmerizing gaze. Forced herself to check out the rest of the fancy gala, and the fancier people, she was currently stuck in the middle of. And the people were fancy, some of the fanciest she'd ever seen. Even he—of their own volition, her eyes moved back to Tall, Dark and Much Too Handsome— was fancy, in his five-thousand-dollar tuxedo and the flashing diamonds on his cuff links. She couldn't hope to compare.

Not that she wanted to. This was *so* not her scene, and once she'd paid her dues, her boss would recognize that fact and move her somewhere else. Somewhere where she could actually make a difference to the world. After all, what did it matter if the wife of the mayor of San Diego was wearing Manolos or Louboutins on her dainty, pampered feet?

It mattered too much, she told herself wryly as she looked around the crowded ballroom. To a lot of people, it mattered too much. Which was why, on her next sweep of the room, she made herself take her time, made herself study—and identify—each face that passed by. As she did, she didn't know whether to be pleased or horrified that she recognized nearly every person there. It was her job, after all, and it was nice to know that the hours she'd spent poring over old newspaper articles and photos hadn't gone to waste.

After all, unlike the rest of the people here, her role wasn't to drink champagne and drop a lot of money on the charity auction. No, her role, her *job*, was to stay on guard and pay attention to what everyone else was doing so she could write all about it when she got home. If she was lucky—if she kept her eyes open and her mouth shut—and the stars actually aligned, someone would say or do something really scandalous or important and she'd have the chance to write about that instead of the food, the wine and whatever designer was currently "it" among Southern California's social elite.

And if she wasn't lucky, well then she still had to pay attention. Still needed to record who was dating whom and who had made a fashion faux pas and who hadn't…

And yes, her job as the society-page reporter for the local paper really was as boring as it sounded. She tried not to let herself dwell on the fact that she'd spent four years at Columbia's School of Journalism only to end up here. Her father would be *so* proud of her—that is, if he hadn't been killed six months ago while embedded with troops in the Middle East.

A waiter passed by with a tray full of champagne flutes, and she reached out and snagged one of the half-full glasses. Drained it in one long—and hopefully elegant—sip. Then blocked her father's death and disapproval from her mind. She needed to focus on the job at hand. Currently, that job was reporting on this ridiculous affair.

To do her job, though, she needed to blend in with her surroundings. Not that she had much of a chance of actually doing that with her department-store dress and clearance shoes, but she could try. At least until her boss saw the light and took her off this godforsaken beat to put her on something a little more important. And more interesting, she thought, barely smothering yet another yawn as she overheard her fifth conversation of the night about liposuction.

Wanting to free up her hands, she turned to place her glass on the empty tray of yet another passing waiter. As she did, though, her eyes once again met dark green ones. And this time, the man they belonged to was only a couple of feet from her instead of halfway across the crowded ballroom.

She didn't know whether to run or rejoice.

In the end, she did neither. Instead, she just stared—stupefied—up into his too-gorgeous face and tried to think of something to say that wouldn't make her sound like a total moron. It didn't work. Her usually quick mind was a total blank, suddenly filled with nothing but images of him. High cheekbones. Shaggy black hair that fell over his forehead. Wickedly gleaming emerald eyes. Sensuous mouth turned up in a wide, charming smile. Broad shoulders. Lean hips. And tall, so tall that she was forced to look up despite the fact that she stood close to six feet in her four-inch heels.

The word *beautiful* really didn't do him justice. Neither did any other word she could think of at the moment. For a second, she was assailed by the fear that she might actually be drooling over the man, something that had never happened before in her twenty-three years of existence. Then again—she reached a discreet hand up to her chin to double-check and nearly sighed in relief when she found it still dry—she'd never seen a man like this up close before.

Hell, whom was she kidding? she asked herself as her knees trembled for the second time that night. She'd never seen a man like this before ever, in real life or in pictures. And yet, here he was, standing right in front of her, his right hand holdi:.g a glass of champagne that he was quite obviously extending toward her.

"You look thirsty," he said, and—of course— his voice matched the rest of him. Deep and dark and wickedly amused. *So* wickedly amused. Suddenly her knees weren't all that was trembling. Her hand, as it reached for the glass of champagne, was shaking, as well.

What was wrong with her?

Besides the fact that her libido had obviously overpowered her brain? she asked herself viciously. But as she stood there, watching him watch her, she figured she'd better find a way to get her brain functioning again. Because the man obviously wasn't going anywhere until he got a response…even if she had no idea how she was supposed to respond to his observation that she was thirsty…

Eventually, though, her brain, and her sense of humor, kicked in. Thank God. "Funny, I was just thinking the same thing about you." It wasn't the wittiest comeback, but it would do.

"Were you?" His mouth curved in a crooked grin that did something strange to her stomach. "Well, you wouldn't be wrong." Then he lifted his own glass of champagne to his lips and took a deep drink. She watched, mesmerized, for long seconds before she managed to shake herself out of it. Jeez! How far gone was she that even watching him swallow was turning her on? Maybe she should just walk away now and cut her losses while she still could.

Even as the thought came to her, she knew she wouldn't do it. Partly because she wasn't sure her knees would hold her if she tried to walk away and partly…partly because in that moment there was nowhere she'd rather be than right there, smiling up at this charming, beautiful man—and having him smile back at her.

"I'm Nic, by the way," he said, after he'd watched her take a slow, steadying drink from her own glass.

"I'm Desi." She held out her hand. He took it, but instead of shaking her hand as she'd expected, he just held it as he gently stroked his thumb across her palm.

The touch was so soft, so intimate, so not what she'd been expecting, that for long seconds she didn't know what to do. What to say. A tiny voice inside her whispered for her to let go, to step back, to walk away from the attraction that was holding them in thrall. But it was drowned out by the heat, the attraction, the *sizzle* that arced between them like lightning.

"Would you like to dance, Desi?" he asked, taking the glass from her other hand and depositing it on a passing tray.

She should say no. She had a million things to do here tonight and none of those things involved getting swept onto the dance floor by some hot, rich guy who had probably forgotten more about seduction than she'd ever known. But even as the thought occurred to her, even knowing that she might very well get burned before the night was over, she nodded. Then she let him lead her gently toward the center of the room. Playing with fire was a cliché for a reason.

The band was playing a slow song—of course it was—and he pulled her into his arms, started to move her across the crowded floor. He held her closer than was necessary or expected for a first dance between strangers. One hand on her lower back, his fingers curving over the soft swell of her hip. His other hand continuing to hold, continuing to stroke, her own. His hard, strong chest brushing against her own with each step they took. His thighs doing the same.

Deep inside, Desi felt herself melting. Felt herself falling a little more under his spell. She knew it was stupid, ridiculous, *insane*, but for the first time in her life, she didn't care. She didn't care if it was a bad idea to let him touch her. Didn't care if she'd regret it later. Didn't care, even, if she ended up getting in trouble at work because she'd spent time with Nic that she should have spent trying to pry quotes out of the local celebrities. Which, if she stopped to think about it, didn't make sense at all. She was a woman who lived to work, who was dying to make a name for herself as a journalist. The fact that she would put that at risk for a man she'd just met was absurd.

She wasn't that girl, had never been—and never wanted to be—*that girl*. And yet, here she was, moving closer instead of back. Arching forward so that her breasts and her thighs brushed more firmly against him, instead of walking away. Surrendering instead of putting up a fight.

The gleam in Nic's eyes as he looked down at her was as obvious as his rock-hard pelvis pressing against her own. Instead of offending her, it aroused her. Instead of making her scurry for cover, it made her clamor for more.

One night never hurt anyone, after all. And neither did one kiss. Or at least that was her story for this evening and she was sticking to it.

Which was why, after taking a deep breath,

she tightened her hand where it rested against the back of his neck and pulled him forward. Pulled him down, down, down, until their bodies were meshed together and his lips met hers.

Two

She was delicious. It was the only thing Nic Durand could think as his lips met those of the beautiful blonde in his arms. Desi, she'd said her name was, he remembered as he fought to keep from getting completely lost in the feel of her soft hands on his neck and her lush body pressed so tightly against his own.

It was a lot harder not to get lost than it should have been. A lot harder than it had ever been. He'd met—and charmed—a lot of women in his life, but never had he been so affected by one. Never had he come so close to forgetting who and where he was when he was with one—even one as gorgeous, and amusing, as Desi. But here he was, attending his first charity gala since he and his brother had moved the headquarters of their diamond company to San Diego earlier that year, and all he could think about was getting his hands and mouth all over a woman he'd just met.

As second in command of Bijoux, he was in charge of marketing, advertising and public relations. It was his job to come to these ridiculous galas, his job to schmooze and donate pieces to the silent auction in an effort to continue building the philanthropic reputation of the business he and his brother, Marc, had poured their hearts and souls into ever since they'd taken over more than a decade before. The fact that he'd rather just give all that money straight to charity meant nothing. After all, experience had proved that buying seats at boring, trumped-up galas like this one always earned his company good PR. And good PR was the name of the game, especially when you were one of the new kids. And not just any new kid, but one determined to shake up the old system and make things happen. It was the best way to gain access. He'd come here tonight with an agenda—people to meet, business to do—but all it had taken was one look at Desi, one conversation with her, one feel of her pressed against him while dancing, to make all of that fly out the window.

And he didn't give a damn.

It was odd. Crazy, even. But he wasn't going to fight it, he decided as he slid his hand down her spine to rest against her lower back. Not when a simple kiss with her was hotter and more exciting than anything he'd done with any other woman.

With that thought in mind, he put a little pressure on her back, pressed her forward…and more tightly against him. She moaned a little at the contact, her mouth opening with the sound, and he took instant advantage by licking his way across the little dip in her upper lip, then across the soft fullness of her lower one. She gasped a little, her hands sliding up to clutch at his tuxedo shirt. It was all the invitation he needed.

Delving inside her then, he swept his tongue along her own. Once, twice, then again and again. Teasing, touching, *tasting* her. Learning her flavors…and her secrets.

Despite her sharp cool looks—all platinum-blond hair and ice-blue eyes, striking cheek-bones and long, slender body—Desi was heat and spice. Cinnamon and cloves, overlaid by just a hint of the crisp, sweet champagne they had shared. The warmth of her seduced him, drew him in—drew him under—until all he could think of, all he could want, was her.

Sliding his other hand into her hair, he tangled his fingers in the silky strands and tugged gently. Her head tilted back in response, giving him better access to her mouth. And he took it without a thought to anything but how much he wanted her.

Sucking her lower lip between his teeth, he bit down gently, then soothed the small hurt with his tongue before once again licking inside her mouth. This time, he slid his tongue along her upper lip, toyed gently with the sensitive skin then delved deep into the recesses of her mouth.

Desi moaned, burrowing even closer as he licked his way across the roof of her mouth before tangling his tongue with hers. She tasted so good, felt so good, that he wanted nothing more than to stay right there forever.

But at that moment someone jostled him. The jolt broke the spell and he came back to himself slowly, became aware of their surroundings and the fact that he was about two seconds from undressing her in the middle of one of the most important social events of the Southern California season. He should be embarrassed, or at least shocked that he'd let things get so far out of hand. But he didn't care about that, didn't care about any of the people milling around them or what they must be thinking.

All he cared about was getting Desi out of there…and getting inside her as quickly as he possibly could.

Pulling away from her reluctantly, he forced himself to ignore her moan of protest—and the way it shot straight to his groin. It wasn't easy. Just as it wasn't easy to look away from her flushed cheeks, her swollen lip and slumberous eyes. But if he didn't, he would say to hell with social niceties and take her right here in the middle of the dance floor where everyone could see them. Where everyone could watch as he put his claim on her.

Just the thought—which was an admittedly odd one to have when he didn't know this woman at all—had him placing a hand on her lower back and escorting her through the bright crowds to the darkness of the balcony beyond the ballroom. As he did, he tried to ignore the looks they were getting. It wasn't easy, especially when he saw the way so many of the men were looking at them. Looking at her. Only the awareness that he was one small step away from growling and beating his chest like some kind of caveman kept him moving.

Desi went with him willingly, pliantly even, which soothed some of the strangely possessive feelings rocketing through him. But he'd barely gotten her outside—the door was still closing behind them—before she was on him. Her arms wrapping around his neck, her body wrapping itself around his own, her mouth desperately seeking his.

The same urgency was a fire inside him. A

pounding drum in his bloodstream, a stroke of lightning that he couldn't shake. That he didn't want to shake.

All he wanted was her.

It was a shocking revelation, and a humbling one. He loved women, loved everything about them and always had. But this driving desire for Desi, this craving to have her any and every way he could, was something new. Something as unexpected as it was exciting.

Keeping his mouth on hers and his lips open so she could delve inside him the same way he had explored her, Nic turned them until her back was against the outside wall of the ballroom. She moaned softly as her bare skin came in contact with the building and he shifted back, so that he could slide an arm between her and the rough, cold stone.

"Please," she whimpered, pressing her pelvis against his as her hands clutched his shirt, pulling and tugging at it in a frantic need that mirrored his own.

To help her—and to get her hands on his bare skin faster—he pulled away slightly and ripped his shirt straight down in a practiced move that had the studs giving way to his impatience. Desi sighed then, her hands sliding beneath the parted fabric to caress his ribs, his back, his abdomen.

Her fingers felt so good—*she* felt so good—that for long seconds he did nothing but stand there, letting her explore him as he longed to explore her. But in the end, his need got the better of him and he took control, pulling the top of her dress down so he could see and touch and kiss her.

"Hey!" she protested breathlessly. "I wasn't done yet."

"I'm sorry," he told her as he gazed at the sun-kissed skin he had revealed. She wasn't wearing a bra, but then she didn't need one. Her breasts were small and high and perfect, tipped with pale pink nipples he was dying to taste. "I promise, you can touch me anywhere you want. Later. Right now, I have to—" His voice trailed off as he pressed hot, openmouthed kisses to her neck, her collarbone and the slope of her shoulder before moving on to her breasts.

Her skin was as soft and fragrant as he'd imagined it would be, and as he pulled her nipple into his mouth, as he circled her areola with his tongue and sucked just hard enough to have her crying out as she buried her hands in his hair, he felt as if he would die if he didn't have her. Soon.

"I need to be inside you," he growled against her breast.

"Yes," she gasped, her hands sliding from his hair to his shoulders, then down his chest to his waist, where she began fumbling with his belt buckle. "Now."

They were the two most beautiful words he'd ever heard.

He slipped a hand under the silky blue skirt of her dress, then slid his fingers up her thigh until he found her underwear—and more important, her sex. He traced the elastic leg of her panties for a few seconds, reveling in the feel of her. Soft. Wet. Hot. So hot that it took all his self-control not to plunge inside her right then.

Still, he couldn't resist slipping two fingers inside the lace.

Couldn't resist petting and stroking her until

her knees buckled and she grabbed at him for
support.

Couldn't resist slipping first one finger and
then another into her tight, silky heat and pressing deep.

"Nic!" It was part command, part plea and in
those moments he wanted—needed—nothing
more than to give her what she was demanding
of him. But first—

He ripped the fragile lace away from her body
with one strong tug, then dropped to his knees
in front of her.

"Oh, yes," she cried, her hands grabbing him
as he lifted one of her legs over his shoulder and,
in doing so, opened her completely to his eyes
and hands and mouth. Then he leaned forward
and blew a long, slow, steady stream of air right
against her most sensitive spot.

She cried out then, a high-pitched strangled
sound that made his own need skyrocket. But
this wasn't just about him, wasn't some quick,
anonymous screw. Not to him anyway. And
though he didn't yet know what it was about Desi
that intrigued him, he did know that he wanted

to see her again. Did know that he wanted to get to know more about her than what color her nipples were or how hot and wet and tight she felt around his finger.

Although he was good with knowing all that, too. More than good, he admitted to himself as he worked his way across her flat stomach, kissing and licking and sucking every inch of her skin.

Her hands moved from his shoulders to his head, her fingers tangling in his hair with a sharpness that only turned him on more. Pleasure coursed through him and he groaned at the sensation before nipping sharply at her hip bone in retaliation.

She cried out again, wobbled a little, then grabbed on to him, her fingers digging into his shoulders as she fought to stay upright. Her obvious arousal fed his, and he gently bit her a second time. A third time. Then he laved the little stings and explored more of her soft, gorgeous skin. As he did, he couldn't help wondering if he'd left marks. If she would look in the mirror tomorrow and see tiny bruises on her hips, her stomach, her thighs, and think of him as he knew—even now—that he'd be thinking of her.

"Please, please, please," she whimpered in the sexiest mantra he'd ever heard. He laughed in response, then kissed his way back across her stomach, then lower, so that his tongue traced along the very edges of her sex.

She was shaking, her body and arms curving around him as much for support as to hold him to her. He loved the feel of her wrapped around him, loved the fact that she was as affected by what was happening between them as he was.

In answer to her silent pleas, he moved closer, pressed her legs apart a little more as he trailed his mouth lower. In response, she stroked her fingers down his face, rubbed the stubble on his jaw. She played with it for long seconds, and her fingers felt so good he felt his resolve crumble. He wanted to be inside her, *needed* to be inside her with a desperation that bordered on insanity.

But he wanted this more. It was a driving compulsion, this need to watch her while she came. To know what she looked like, sounded like, tasted like when he took her to the edge and then flung her over.

With that thought a beacon shining through his own dark and desperate need, he leaned forward and put his mouth on her. Then he nearly lost it as Desi pressed a hand against her mouth to muffle her scream.

She was in sensory overload, her every nerve popping with pleasure at the feel of Nic touching her. At the feel of his arm around her waist, his big, calloused hand kneading her backside. At the feel of his fingers still buried deep inside her. At the feel and sound and sight of his mouth moving against her sex.

It was so good, *so good*, that she couldn't stop herself from pressing back against the wall, against his hand, even as she tilted her hips forward to give him better access.

She was so close that it didn't take long to bring her right to the edge. She knew he was aware of how close she was. She could feel it in the tension of his shoulders and in the slow, careful way he caressed her. For a moment, just a moment, she wondered what he was waiting for, but then the insidious pleasure of what he was doing, the care he was taking, streaked through her. Intense, powerful, mind-numbing.

"Nic, I can't—"

"You can," he told her, his voice hoarse with his own restraint.

"I can't," she answered, the words broken and brittle and breathless. "I need—"

"I know what you need." He kissed her then, hot and openmouthed, making her knees tremble and her hands shake. Her whole body slammed into overload and she reached for him, her fingers tugging at his shirt, his hair, the bowtie hanging limply from his collar.

"Please, please, please," she muttered mindlessly as she arched against him. She needed more, needed him.

He cursed then, harsh and low, and the words felt hot against her skin. The sensation only added to the tension inside her until she couldn't think, couldn't see, couldn't breathe. All she could do was feel.

All she could do was crave.

And then he did it. He twisted his fingers inside her even as he swirled his tongue around her most sensitive spot and reached up with his free hand to pinch one of her nipples, hard.

The different sensations slammed Desi into overload. She careened straight over the edge into ecstasy, her body shuddering as pleasure swamped her, more intense and powerful and shattering than anything she had ever felt before.

"Nic!" Lost in the maelstrom, she cried out for him.

And he was there, his hands stroking her soothingly even as he took her higher and higher and higher. Even as he thrust her straight into the stars that shined so brilliantly above them.

When the pleasure broke, when she finally started to come back to herself, Nic wouldn't allow it. Instead, he fumbled with the front of his tuxedo trousers as he shoved to his feet. Then he cupped his hands under her and lifted her right off her feet.

She was still pleasure drunk and more than a little dazed, but even so, her instincts kicked in. She wrapped her legs around his lean waist, her arms around his broad shoulders and pressed back against the wall for better leverage.

Then he was there between her thighs, blunt and hard and big. She had just come, but as he probed gently at her opening, Desi couldn't help but respond.

He had been so patient, so careful to ensure that she was satisfied, that she expected him to be impatient now. To be rough, hurried.

Instead, he took his time here, too. Leaning forward until his lips were right next to her ear, he whispered, "You're so damn beautiful." Then he pressed soft kisses to her cheek.

The words, combined with the feel of him right against the core of her body, took her arousal up another notch. "It's okay," she told him, arching her hips in an effort to encourage him. "I'm ready."

He groaned then, thrusting forward gently until he was buried halfway inside her. "Okay?" he ground out, and she felt him shaking from the effort it took to hold himself back.

Touched more than she wanted to be—certainly more than she'd expected to be from a torrid encounter with a stranger—she leaned into him. Pressed her mouth to his in a kiss as soft and gentle as his concern for her. "Please," she whispered against his lips. "I want to feel you inside me."

That whisper was all it took to snap his control like a twig—which she was exceptionally grateful for.

Nic thrust into her then, so hard that he slammed her back against the wall. But she was still wet, still turned-on, and more than ready for him. Pleasure crashed through her at the first stroke, coursing along her every nerve ending until her entire body felt lit up like the Fourth of July.

"Damn!" he growled, his fingers digging into her hips as he held her in place. "You feel good."

Again, she expected him to slam into her, even braced herself for it, but again he surprised her. He brushed kisses across her forehead, her cheeks, her lips as he waited for her to adjust to him. Only when she squirmed against him, trying to get closer, did he finally relent.

He began to move in slow, steady, powerful

strokes that had her grasping at him as the need ratcheted up inside her. Soon—too soon—she was on the brink of coming again. But she didn't want to go over alone this time, didn't want to lose herself in the ecstasy without him.

Tightening her inner muscles in a long, slow caress, she did what she could to take him as high as he had taken her. She brushed her thumbs across his nipples, whispered how much she wanted him in his ear, lifted her hips to meet each of his thrusts. It must have worked, because he groaned, then began thrusting harder.

Then he was leaning forward, his mouth inches from hers. "Kiss me," he commanded, a scant moment before his lips slammed down on hers.

She did, pulling his lower lip between her teeth and nipping at him as he had done to her earlier. She wanted more of him, wanted all of him. Craved him until it was an inferno deep inside her.

She bit him again, a little harder this time, and the shock of pain must have been what he was waiting for, because he came with a growl. She tore her mouth away from his, gasped for breath, but Nic wouldn't let her go. He followed her, his mouth ravenous on her own while the heat of his body seared hers wherever it touched. In moments, the pleasure swamped her, overwhelmed her, and she followed him over the edge, her body spinning wildly, gloriously, completely out of her control.

Three

When it was over, when she could breathe again and her scattered thoughts finally came back to her, Desi didn't know what to do. What to say. How to act.

There was a part of her that was shell-shocked. A part of her that couldn't believe she had just had sex with a stranger *in public*. And not just in public, but on the balcony outside a gala that she was supposed to be covering for work. If someone had told her an hour ago that before the night was over she'd be pressed up against the hotel's outside wall, her legs wrapped around Nic, whose last name she didn't even know, having just had the most intense orgasms of her life… Well, she wouldn't have called that person a liar. She would have called him or her a *damn* liar and then laughed herself silly.

But here she was. And the kicker was, she wasn't even sorry. How could she be when her body was so blissed out that she still wasn't sure her legs would be able to hold her when Nic decided to set her down? Which—thankfully—he hadn't yet made any move to do.

"You okay?" he asked after a minute, pressing his lips to her neck.

"I don't know. That was—" Her voice broke and she swallowed in an effort to get some moisture into her too-dry throat.

"Amazing," he said, kissing his way over her collarbone. "Incredible. Earth-shattering."

She giggled. It was a totally foreign sound to her, one Desi couldn't ever remember making in her adult life. She wasn't the giggling sort. Then again, she wasn't the one-night-stand, public-sex-against-a-building sort, either. And yet here she was, with absolutely no desire to move. And absolutely no regrets.

Nic lifted his head, gave her a mock frown that in no way reached the beautiful green eyes she could just barely make out in the shadows. "Are you saying that making love to me wasn't earth-shattering?"

He slipped a hand between them, circled his thumb around her. She gasped, arched against him. She knew exactly what he was doing, knew that he was teasing her, but she couldn't help it. Normally, she never let a man get the upper hand, but with Nic she couldn't help it. Everything about him appealed to her, drew a response from her that she had almost no control over. His sense of humor, the intelligence she could see in his eyes, the careful way he held and touched and kissed her. And, of course, the fact that he was the hottest man she had ever met certainly didn't hurt, either.

"I'm saying," she said, her voice more breathless than she would have liked, "that I very much enjoyed having sex with you."

"Sex, huh?" He rubbed a little harder, a little faster, and shocks of electricity sparked through her. Just that easily, he made her ache. Made her want. Again.

"Nic," she whispered, cupping the back of his neck with her palm, even as her head fell back against the cool stucco wall.

"Desi." His voice was low, teasing, but she could hear the sudden thread of tension as clearly as she could feel him hardening once again within her.

"Don't play." Suddenly she was as needy, as desperate, as if she hadn't come at all.

He scraped his teeth along her jaw, bit lightly at the sensitive spot behind her ear. "I thought you liked it when I played." His breath was hot against her skin, the words a whisper that worked its way deep inside of her.

"You know what I mean." She clenched her core around him to underscore her words, took great delight in the sexy hiss the movement elicited from him. He closed his eyes, dropped his forehead against hers, and the hungry noise he made had her tightening her inner muscles again and again.

He cursed then, a harsh, sexy word that only

ramped up her arousal more. From the moment he'd taken her out onto this balcony—hell, from the moment he'd kissed her on that dance floor— Nic had had the upper hand. She'd be lying if she said it didn't feel good to get a little of her own back. Especially when doing so was so incredibly pleasurable for both of them.

Nic's hand tightened on her behind as he lifted her nearly off him before letting her slowly sink back down. He did it a second time and then a third, all the while continuing to stroke her with his other hand. It took only a minute or two before ecstasy beckoned—brought even closer by his careless demonstration of strength—but just as she was about to go over the edge for the third time in less than an hour, he stilled.

"What's wrong?" She forced open her too-heavy lids, tried to focus on his face despite the urgent need lighting her up from the inside. "Why'd you stop?'

"Come home with me."

"What?" She was so far gone that her brain had trouble assimilating his words.

"Come home with me," he repeated, thrusting deep inside her for emphasis. She moaned despite herself, tried to arch against him and get that last bit of needed pressure. But he held her firmly, refused to let her move. Refused to let her come.

"Please," she gasped, her whole body shaking with the need for release. "I need—"

"I know what you need," he whispered, taking her mouth in a kiss that was somehow both hard and tender. "Say you'll go home with me and I'll let you come."

She bit his lip, not hard enough to draw blood but definitely hard enough to make him take notice. "Let me come," she countered breathlessly, "and maybe I'll go home with you."

He laughed then, a low, dark sound that sent shivers down her spine even as it made her entire body melt. "I want you in my bed."

She tightened around him yet again, taking great pleasure in the fact that he groaned deep in his throat. "You know what you need to do then."

"Is that a yes?" He stroked her once gently.

Too gently, but she wasn't complaining as her nerve endings tingled.

"It's not a no."

He laughed again. "Damn, I like you, Desi."

"I certainly hope you do, considering what we've spent the last forty-five minutes doing." She had to bite her tongue, but somehow she managed to resist adding that she liked him, too. A lot. She hadn't been with that many men— only two before Nic—but neither of them had ever made her laugh. Not out of bed and certainly not while making love to her. Until him, until *now*, she hadn't even known that she'd been missing something.

He bent his head, licking his way over first one nipple and then the other. "Come home with me," he urged when she was even more of a trembling, needy mess, "and I'll spend the rest of the night showing you just how much I like you."

She didn't want to give in—not because she didn't like him, but because she did. Too much. And the last thing she needed right now was to fall for a sexy, charismatic rich guy who would break her heart if she let him.

And yet…and yet, like him, she wasn't quite ready for this night to end. Wasn't quite ready to walk away from Nic with his bright green eyes and ready smile, his quick wit and gentle hands. And she sure as hell wasn't ready to walk away from the pleasure he brought her so effortlessly.

"Please, Desi," he murmured against her cheek, and for the first time she heard the strain in his voice, felt it in the way he trembled against her. "I want you," he said. "If you just want it to be tonight, that's okay with me. But please—"

"Okay." In one desperate, vulnerable moment, she threw caution to the wind.

"Okay?"

"I'll come home with you."

His eyes shot up to hers. "You will?"

"I will." She grinned a little wickedly herself. "That is, if you make me come in the next sixty seconds." This might be her first—and probably her last—one-night stand, but that didn't mean she couldn't make the best of it…

"I thought you'd never ask." His answering

smile was blinding, and it caught her right in the gut. Which probably would have made her nervous if her body hadn't been on a collision course with its third orgasm of the night.

Nic bent down and took her mouth with his. Less than thirty seconds later he was muffling her screams as she came and came and came.

His house was gorgeous. Worse, it was perfect. Which, she was growing desperately afraid, was simply a reflection of its owner. And while most women would jump at the shot to start something with a gorgeous, rich, *perfect* man, Desi wasn't most women. The thought of falling for Nic made her itch, so much so that she couldn't help casting a few surreptitious glances down at her bare legs to make sure she wasn't actually breaking out in hives.

Which was why it made absolutely no sense that she was sitting at the bar in the middle of Nic's (still didn't know his last name and still didn't want to) gorgeously designed arts-and-crafts kitchen at two in the morning, watching as he made her homemade blueberry pancakes.

Simply because he'd asked what her favorite food was and that was what she had answered.

"So, what's your favorite TV show?" he questioned as he expertly flipped the first batch of pancakes. Watching him made her a little crazy, especially since all he had on was a pair of well-worn jeans. No man should be allowed to look that good outside the pages of a fashion magazine.

And no man should be able to make pancakes that perfect after three rounds of the best, most earth-shattering sex she had ever engaged in. It went against the laws of nature.

"Desi?" he prompted, casting a quick glance over his shoulder at her.

She tried to look as if she hadn't spent the past ten minutes ogling his perfectly defined back. Judging from the smirk on his face, she didn't succeed nearly as well as she'd hoped to.

So she cleared her throat and focused on answering his question as a means of distraction from the fact that she was more than a little afraid that she was turning into a sex addict. "I don't watch TV."

"What do you mean you don't watch TV?" He turned to stare at her incredulously. *"Everyone* watches TV."

She quirked a brow at him. "Not everyone. Obviously."

He named a few popular shows, but when she just shook her head, Nic sighed heavily. "Okay, fine. How about your favorite movie, then? Or do you not watch movies, either?"

"I watch movies. But it's hard to pick just one, isn't it?" She did her best to keep from smiling at his obvious frustration.

"Not necessarily."

"Oh, yeah? What's your favorite then?"

"Titanic."

It was her turn to stare at him incredulously. "You don't really mean that, right? You're just messing with me. You have to be."

"Why wouldn't I mean it?" He looked completely disgruntled now. "It's a fantastic movie. Love, passion, danger, excitement. What's not to like?"

"Oh, I don't know. Betrayal, maybe? Attempted suicide, attempted murder, poverty, *icebergs,* death. Not to mention the world's most infamous sinking ship." She paused as if considering. "You're right. What was I thinking? It's a barrel of laughs. Obviously."

He made a disgusted sound. "You're a real party pooper. Did anyone ever tell you that?"

"No."

"Well, then, let me be the first. You're a real party pooper."

"I'm a realist."

He snorted. "You're a nihilist."

She started to argue on general principle, but stopped before she could do more than utter a few incoherent sounds. After all, whom was she kidding? He was totally right. "Just call me Camus," she quipped with a shrug.

"Is that a movie?" he asked as he poured more batter on the griddle.

"Are you serious?" she demanded, watching him like a hawk as she tried to find some kind of tell to prove he was messing with her. But the look he sent her was utterly guileless. Not too guileless, mind you. Just guileless enough, as if he really had no idea what she was talking about.

Huh. Maybe he wasn't so perfect, after all. The thought made her inexplicably happy, though she refused to delve too deeply into why that was.

"Albert Camus was a French writer," she told him after a second.

"Oh." He shrugged. "Never heard of him."

That knowledge made her infinitely more relaxed. "Oh, well, a lot of people would say you weren't missing much."

"But not you."

"Maybe. Maybe not."

He grinned as he slid a plate piled high with perfect, golden, fluffy pancakes in front of her. "But you still didn't tell me what your favorite movie is."

"I told you I couldn't choose just one. Not all of us can wax poetic over a sinking boat, after all."

"More's the pity." He cast her a mischievous look that she immediately mistrusted. "But you know what? I think you're right. I don't think I can choose just one favorite movie. Now that I'm thinking about it, a few more come to mind."

"Oh yeah? Like what?"

"*The Stranger*, definitely. And maybe *The Guest*. And—"

"You suck!" she told him, breaking off a piece of pancake and throwing it at him. He caught it, of course. In his mouth. Without even trying. "Those are two of Albert Camus's most famous works."

"Are they?" he asked, his face a mask of complete and total innocence. "I had no idea."

She studied him closely, looking for his tell. He was lying to her, obviously, but the fact that she couldn't tell was odd. She could always tell— she prided herself on it. It's what made her such a good investigative journalist. And such a lousy society columnist.

The fact that he didn't seem to have a tell fascinated her. And made her very, very nervous all at the same time.

When she didn't say anything else, he nodded at her untouched plate. "Eat your pancakes before they get cold."

"Maybe I like cold pancakes."

"Do you?"

"I don't know. Do I?"

He didn't answer. Instead he grabbed the bottle of maple syrup and drizzled it over the top of her pancakes. Then he cut into them and lifted a forkful to her mouth.

He waited patiently for a few seconds, but when she just looked at him instead of taking the proffered bite, he rolled his eyes. "*My* pancakes don't taste good cold. Trust me."

Trust him. The idea was so ludicrous that she nearly laughed out loud. Only the knowledge that he definitely wouldn't get the joke kept her from making one wisecrack or another. But there was no way in hell she was *ever* going to trust *him*. Mr. Perfect. No, thank you. Been there, done that, still had the T-shirt as a not-so-pleasant memento.

Not that she was bitter or anything. Or sexist.

Because it wasn't that she didn't trust men. It was that she didn't trust *anybody*. Not when life had taught her over and over *and over* again that she couldn't count on anyone or anything. If she needed something, she could count on only herself to make it happen. Anyone else would just let her down.

Maybe it wasn't a great philosophy, and maybe—just maybe—it *was* a touch nihilistic. But it was *her* philosophy. She'd lived by it most of her life, and while it hadn't gotten her much—yet—it also hadn't cost her much since she'd adopted it. And in her mind, that was a win.

And yet, even understanding all that, she—inexplicably—leaned forward and let Nic feed her the bite of pancake. She had no idea why she did it, but it certainly wasn't because doing so made him look incredibly happy. Not at all. Not even a little bit.

That was her story, and like her philosophy, she was sticking to it.

Which was why it was so strange when, after she finished chewing, Nic simply handed her the fork and went back to what he was doing without so much as a backward glance. Was she the only one affected by this strange night of theirs?

It was a definite possibility, she told herself. He could totally be the kind of guy who picked up a different one-night stand at every party he went to. Which would mean that tonight—hot sex and cool banter and delicious pancakes—

could be standard operating procedure for him. Which was fine, she told herself, despite the sinking feeling in her stomach. One-night stands weren't SOP for her—far from it—but that was what she'd expected, what she'd wanted, when she'd come home with him. Deciding in the middle of it that she wanted something more wasn't okay, no matter how much pleasure he gave her or how much she enjoyed sitting here, teasing him.

"So, favorite movie is off the table," he said, after he poured another round of pancakes onto the griddle. "How about favorite song?"

She forked up another bite of pancakes under his watchful eye, took her time chewing it. "What's with all the questions?" she asked after she finally swallowed it.

"What's with all the evasive answers?" he countered.

"I asked you first."

"Actually, if you think about it, I asked you first. About your favorite song. And I'm still waiting."

"You are a persistent one," she said, narrowing her eyes at him.

"I believe the word you're looking for is *charming*." He crossed to the fridge, took out a bottle of champagne and a quart of fresh-squeezed orange juice. "*Debonair*. Maybe even…*sexy*?"

He wiggled his brows at her then, and it took every ounce of concentration she had not to burst out laughing. "Sexy, hmm. Maybe. And here I was thinking *humble*."

"Well, obviously. Being humble is what PR professionals the world over are known for."

"Is that what you are?" she asked, intrigued by the rare glimpse into his real life. "A public relations guy?" It would explain the gorgeous house and even more gorgeous artisan decorating scheme.

He shrugged. "In a manner of speaking."

"That isn't an answer."

He faked a surprised look as he slid a mimosa in front of her. "You don't actually think you're the only one who can dodge questions here, do you?"

She did laugh then. She couldn't help it. He

really was the most charming and interesting man she had met in a very long time. Maybe ever.

She reached for the champagne flute he'd put in front of her and took a long sip. As she did, Nic took advantage of her preoccupation and grabbed her smartphone off the counter.

"What are you doing?" she demanded as he started pressing keys.

"Programming my number into it, so you can call me whenever you want."

"What makes you think I'm going to want to call you when tonight is over?"

He gave her what she guessed was his most unassuming look. "What makes you think you aren't?"

"Are we seriously going to spend the rest of the night asking each other questions and never getting any answers?"

"I don't know. Are we?"

She rolled her eyes in exasperation. But before she could say anything else, his phone started buzzing from where it sat next to the stove. He made no move to answer it.

"Aren't you going to get that?" she asked, partly because the reporter in her wanted to know who was calling him at two-thirty in the morning and partly because he was standing just a little too close to her. They weren't touching, but she could feel the heat emanating from his body, and it was making it impossible for her to think—and even more impossible for her to maintain the distance she was trying so desperately to cling to.

"It's just me, calling from your phone. So now I've got your number, too." He looked her in the eye when he said it and there was something in that look, something in his voice, that made her think he meant a lot more than the ten digits that made her phone ring.

Suddenly she was taking far too much effort not to squirm.

She didn't like the feeling any more than she liked the vulnerability that came with the knowledge that he could see more of her than she wanted him to. And so she did what she always did in situations like these—she went on the offensive. "What if I hadn't planned on giving you my number?"

He raised a brow. "You don't want me to have it?"

"That's not the point!"

"It's exactly the point."

"No, it—" She cut herself off. "You're a piece of work, you know that?"

"I have been told that a time or two." He paused, then said, "So I've got a proposition for you."

"Uh, no, thanks." She moved to stand up, but he pressed her back into the seat.

"You haven't even heard what I was going to say."

"Yeah, well, when a guy says those words to a girl he hardly knows, it usually ends with her chained in a basement somewhere while he maps out patterns to make a dress from her skin."

"Wow!" He cracked up. "Suspicious much?"

"I've seen *Silence of the Lambs*. I know how these things work."

"It appears that you do. But, sadly, I have no basement. And no handcuffs. And no deep-seated psychopathology, at least not that I know of. Also, I don't have a clue how to sew. So, you're probably safe."

"I'll be the judge of that." She eyed him with mock suspicion. "So what exactly is this proposition of yours?"

"That I keep your phone number, even though you aren't exactly overjoyed that I've got it. And I promise that I won't call you until you call me first. Fair?"

"What if I never call you?"

"Then I'll be very sad, but I promise I won't bother you with harassing phone calls. Deal?"

She thought about it for a moment, thought about whether or not she would ever want to talk to him again once this night was over. And decided, what the hell. She might as well leave the option open. If she didn't want to use it, well, then, he was giving her the perfect opportunity to walk away, no harm, no foul.

"Deal," she told him.

"Excellent." He smiled, then reached a hand up to rub the back of his neck. Involuntarily, her eyes were drawn to his very enticing six-pack and the V-cut that peeked out of the top of his low-slung jeans. She locked her jaw and, for the second time that night, tried not to drool.

She must not have been very successful, though, because his voice was amused a few seconds later when he asked, "See something you like?"

"I like you." The words were out before she had a clue she was going to say them. The second it registered that she'd actually spoken what she'd only planned to think, she clapped her hand over her mouth in horror.

She wanted to take them back, wanted to pretend she hadn't just screwed up everything by letting her tongue—and her emotions—get away from her. But it was too late. The words hung there in the air between them, like a bomb waiting to go off.

He didn't look horrified by her admission, though. Didn't look as if he was about to duck and cover in an effort to avoid the shrapnel from the bomb she had just dropped. In fact, Nic looked absolutely delighted, as though she'd given him a present…or the best orgasm of his life.

Which wasn't so far-fetched when she thought about it. He'd certainly done that for her, after all.

Before she could think of something—anything—to say that might work as damage control, he closed the small distance between them. He turned her stool around so that she was facing him, then moved closer still, until he was nestled between the V of her spread legs.

"I like you, too," he said, pressing a kiss to her forehead, then another one to her cheek and yet another one to her lips.

"Do you?" she asked, tilting her head back so he could skim his lips along the side of her neck.

"I do. And since we've established that you like me as well…" His hands went to the buttons of the too-big shirt she was wearing. His shirt, she thought dazedly as he slipped the first two buttons through their holes then gently skimmed his knuckles along the undersides of her breasts. "I think we should maybe head back to my bedroom and like each other some more."

"Like each other some more?" she repeated, trying to keep her voice steady despite the heat arcing through her like a lightning storm. "Is that what they're calling it these days?"

He laughed. "It's what I'm calling it. Sorry. I know it's not very romantic, but my brain pretty much stops working the second I touch you."

She was charmed by the admission despite herself. Determined to keep things light after the confession she'd had no intention of making, she told him, "I guess it's all right if your brain isn't working, as long as other parts of your anatomy are."

He quirked a brow at her. "The other parts of my anatomy are working just fine, thank you very much."

"Oh, yeah?" She ran a hand over his firm, hard chest. "Prove it."

His eyes darkened at the challenge and he grabbed her hips. Pulled her forward until she was balanced right on the edge of the seat and her sex was nestled right up against the hard ridge of his erection.

"Proof enough for you?" he whispered, his breath hot against her ear.

"I don't know. I think I might need a more detailed demonstration." She arched against him then, reveling in the groan he didn't even try to hold back.

"A more detailed demonstration, hmm?" He slid his hands under her and picked her up as if she weighed nothing. For the second time that night, Desi wound her arms and legs around him.

She clung to him like a limpet as he carried her out of the kitchen, through the family room and down the long hallway that led to his bedroom. She waited until he'd crossed over the threshold before she leaned forward and whispered in his ear, "'Need You Tonight.'"

"I need you, too," he said as he carried her over to the bed.

It was her turn to laugh. "I meant, that's my favorite song."

Something moved in his eyes—something wonderful and terrifying and so, so exhilarating. Then he was kissing her, his mouth slamming down on hers with the same desperation that was suddenly crashing through her.

And then they were falling onto the bed with him on top of her.

"What's *your* favorite song?" she managed to choke out as he finished unbuttoning her shirt, pressing kisses to each new bit of exposed skin. Her brain was going fast, her body taking over, but after all the back-and-forth, she wanted— needed—to know this one thing about him.

"I thought that was obvious," he said and she could feel him smile against her stomach. "Eric Clapton's 'Wonderful Tonight.'"

Four

Nic woke up alone. Which was unexpected. And which also really, really sucked.

Especially since it wasn't as if Desi was temporarily gone, like in the kitchen making coffee or the bathroom taking a shower. No, she had bugged out of his place and taken every last trace of her existence with her. She hadn't left a note, hadn't left a last name, hadn't left so much as a high-heeled glass slipper behind for him to go by.

She was *really* gone. So gone that if he didn't have scratches down his back from her nails, a bed that looked like a disaster zone, and—he glanced at his phone, just to make sure—her phone number in his contacts list, he might be tempted to think he'd imagined the whole damn thing.

But he hadn't imagined it. Desi was real. He had her number to prove it, he told himself as he stared at the 323 area code of his last missed call. Unfortunately, he also had a promise—not to use that phone number until she used his first.

Which, again, really, really sucked.

Because he liked her. He really, really liked her. More than should be possible considering he knew almost nothing about her—and what knowledge he did have, he'd gained from asking questions and pushing the issue until she very reluctantly responded.

Which, now that he thought about it, probably should have been his first clue that this wasn't going to go the way he'd wanted it to. Damn it, he really hated playing the fool.

A quick look at his bedside clock told him it was barely 7:00 a.m., and since he knew she'd been asleep in his bed at five, when he'd finally succumbed to exhaustion, he couldn't shake the idea that he had just missed her. That if only he had woken up a few minutes earlier, he would have caught her before she disappeared.

The thought made him crazy, especially since he'd planned on starting the morning the same way he'd spent most of the night. Deep inside Desi, watching her fall apart, as the defensive wall she'd built around herself crumbled one tiny brick at a time.

It seemed like a ridiculous plan now, considering he was alone in rapidly cooling sheets. After all, he'd known she was emotionally closed off—he would have had to be an idiot not to see the No Trespassing signs she had posted over pretty much every part of herself. And yet…and yet she'd opened up to him, over and over again through the night. Oh, not about big things such as who she was or why she had such a bleak outlook on people or even what her favorite movie was. But she'd let her guard down enough for him to catch glimpses of a lot of the mixed-up pieces that made her who she was.

He'd liked what he'd seen, a lot. Which was just one more reason this disappearing act of hers bothered him so much. For the first time in a very long time, he'd been looking forward to exploring her. To exploring *them* and finding out all the little things that made Desi tick.

For God's sake, he'd brought her to his *house*, which was something he did not normally do. At least not until he'd been on a few dates with a woman. And definitely not until he knew she was someone he wanted to get serious with.

Yet last night, on that balcony, he'd been adamant about convincing Desi to come home with him. True, part of that was because he'd really, really wanted to sleep with her again—the two times on the balcony hadn't been close to enough to exhaust the sexual chemistry between them. But that didn't explain why he'd been so determined to bring her home, to his house. They'd been at a hotel, for God's sake. How much easier would it have been to simply stop by the front desk and get a room for the night?

Instead, he'd brought her home. He'd made her blueberry pancakes and asked her questions and—when she had commented on various pieces of his furniture—had even thought about showing her his studio, which was pretty much the most sacred place in his house. He barely let his brother, Marc, in there, let alone anyone else.

But she didn't know any of that, a part of him rationalized. He'd thought he had made his interest clear to her last night, but maybe he hadn't. Maybe she'd thought she really was nothing more than a one-night stand to him. Maybe she'd thought he expected her to be gone when he woke up. After all, he hadn't said otherwise.

No, but he'd made a point of giving her his phone number, he told himself as he rolled out of bed and padded into the bathroom. Had made a point of getting hers. Surely that had given her a clue that he was interested in her.

Then again, maybe his interest—or lack thereof—wasn't the problem. Maybe hers was. She'd been pretty damn reluctant to answer even his most innocuous questions, and when she had answered, it was usually with a non-answer. As if she was afraid of letting him too close, of letting him learn too much about her. Or maybe, more accurately, she didn't want him to get close to her.

Just the thought annoyed him. It had been a long time since he'd met a woman who really interested him. Who was smart and funny and also sexy as hell. So why was it that the first woman he did meet who interested him on all those fronts had gone running from him the first chance she'd gotten?

He turned on the shower, and while he was waiting for it to warm up, he took a long, hard look at himself in the mirror. As he did, he couldn't help wondering what it was Desi had seen when she'd looked at him. Had she seen his public persona, the easygoing, happy-go-lucky guy who was always up for a beer or a game of golf? The guy who didn't make waves and always had a joke at the ready?

Or had she seen deeper than that? Had she seen who he really was under all the polish and bull? He'd tried to show her a little bit of that guy last night, had thought—when he caught her looking at him as if she had a million questions—that maybe she had seen him. And if she had…if she had, was that who she had run away from? Not the man she'd picked up at the gala, but the one who lurked below his surface?

The idea grated. But it also lingered, long after he'd all but scrubbed himself raw in the shower in an effort to get rid of the warm-honey scent of her that had somehow embedded itself in his skin.

He was still poking at the wound, still turning it over in his mind, when he cruised into his brother's office an hour later.

"How was the gala?" Marc asked without looking up from where he was checking his first emails of the day.

"Enlightening," Nic answered, walking over to the window that made up one whole wall of the room. Beyond the company grounds were rocky cliffs and a small sandy beach. Beyond that was the endless Pacific. He watched the water for long minutes, saw the waves build out at sea, then crest, then roll harmlessly onto shore. It was winter, so the water was cold, but there were a

few surfers out there, paddling on their boards
as they waited for the next big wave.

For a second, he wanted to be out there with
them. Wanted to be free, wanted—for just once
in his life—to do whatever he wanted. To be
whomever he wanted and to hell with the consequences.

But then Marc asked, "Enlightening how?"
and the fantasy was shattered.

"What do you mean?" He turned to look at
his brother.

Marc pushed back from his desk, then crossed
the room to the small minifridge embedded in
the bar. He grabbed a bottle of iced coffee for
himself, then tossed Nic a pint of the fresh-
squeezed orange juice he favored. He caught it
neatly.

"When I asked you about the gala, you said it
was enlightening. How so?" Marc came to stand
next to him by the window, glancing out at the
ocean before turning to Nic, an inquisitive look
on his face.

Nic started to gloss over it, to focus on the
people he'd met or the money he'd pledged from

Bijoux. But Marc was his brother and his best friend, the only person he ever really opened up to. And so, before Nic even knew the words were there, he found himself saying, "I met a girl."

"You met a *girl*?"

"A woman," he corrected himself, thinking of Desi's lush curves and quick wit. "I met a woman."

"Do tell." Marc gestured to the chair opposite his desk, and though Nic had too much energy to really want to sit, he found himself doing so anyway. As usual.

"What's her name?" his brother asked.

"Desi."

"Desi…?"

"That's all. I don't have her last name."

"Well, that's sloppy on your part." Marc studied him closely. "Which is not an adjective I would usually use to describe you, so… This must be big."

"It's not big. It's not anything, really." And yet Nic really didn't like the way those words tasted in his mouth.

Marc laughed. "Of course not. Which is why

you look like you swallowed a bug just saying that."

"Look, it's complicated."

"Dude, it's always complicated."

"Yeah, well, this time, it's really complicated." And so he told Marc the whole story, about how he'd fallen for Desi's looks at first sight and her startling quick wit almost as fast. About how he'd taken her home…and how he'd woken up alone.

"But you have her phone number, right?" Marc asked when Nic was finished with his tale of woe. "Please, tell me you were smart enough to get her number."

"Of course I was. But I was dumb enough to promise her I wouldn't call her until she called me."

Marc rolled his eyes. "All these years and have I really taught you nothing about how to woo a woman?"

"Considering you've spent the last six years licking your wounds from Isabella, I'd have to say that your own wooing skills are pretty lacking right now."

"I haven't been licking my wounds," Marc growled. "I've been busy running a multi-billion-dollar diamond corporation."

"Yeah, yeah, yeah. Call it whatever you like. Besides, I've been right here with you every step of the way, turning Bijoux into the second-largest responsibly sourced diamond corporation in the world."

"I know that—I wasn't implying otherwise. I was just saying I haven't had much time to woo anyone lately. Then again, neither have you. Maybe you're rusty."

Nic shot him a look. "I am not rusty, thank you very much." Sure, he preferred quality over quantity and always had, despite his playboy image in the press. But it wasn't as if he'd gone months without sex, for God's sake. His skills weren't rusty. At least, he didn't think they were.

God, what if that's why Desi had snuck out before he'd woken up? Because she'd thought he was bad in— No, no, no. That was one rabbit hole he was not going to fall down this morning. Because if he did…hell, if he did, he was afraid he'd never climb back out of it again.

"I'm not rusty," he said again, perhaps with more force than was absolutely necessary.

"I'm not saying you are." Marc held his hands up in mock surrender. "I'm just saying, if you have her phone number, why don't you use it?"

"I already told you—"

"I know. You can't call her until she calls you. But that doesn't mean you can't text her, right? Or did you make promises about that, too? And let me just say, if you did, you're stupider than you look."

"I didn't, actually," Nic answered as the wheels started turning in his brain. "I mean, I suppose an argument could be made about the spirit of the agreement—"

"Screw the spirit of the agreement. You like this woman, right?"

Nic thought of Desi's laugh, the way it filled a room and wrapped itself around him. Thought of her eyes, soft and pleasure dazed and welcoming. "Yeah," he told his brother hoarsely.

"So text her. Make her laugh. You're good at that. Then ask her out."

He nodded. Marc was right. Nic was good at that. He was usually really good at this whole dating thing. So what was it about Desi that threw him so completely off his game? He didn't know, but he figured it was important that she did. And he wanted to find out why he found her so fascinating. Why he'd spent the whole morning thinking about her when she'd made it fairly obvious that she didn't feel the same about him.

"Okay, yeah. I'll do that." He pushed to his feet, pulled his phone from his pocket. "Thanks, man."

Marc laughed. "I didn't mean now! It's barely eight in the morning. Besides, we're both due in a meeting that started five minutes ago."

"I'm not a total idiot, you know. I was just… thinking of what I wanted to say."

His brother came up behind him and clapped him on the back. "Wow, you really do have it bad."

Nic flipped him off as he led the way out of the office and down the hallway to the meeting room—after tucking his phone back in his pants. And if he spent the bulk of the meeting mentally composing a message to Desi, well, nobody needed to know that but him.

Five

"Desi, get in here. I've got a story for you," Malcolm Banks, her boss, called to her from across the newsroom.

"On my way," she answered, grabbing her tablet and heading toward the door with an enthusiasm she was far from feeling.

"Good luck," her friend Stephanie, a junior reporter for the fashion pages, mouthed to her. "Hope it's a good one!"

But Desi just shrugged. This was going to be another society story, she just knew it. She had, in fact, pretty much given up on getting a story of genuine worth anytime in the next decade or so. Because, despite her hard work generating and following up on numerous important story ideas over the past two months, Malcolm refused to give her a chance to write a story that really mattered.

He kept telling her she had to earn her way out of the society pages, and she kept trying. But she was beginning to think that she would be stuck there until she died. Or until Malcolm did, one or the other. Because there was no way she could get a job at another newspaper or magazine, not after she'd spent the past year and a half of her life covering parties and obituaries.

She didn't let her discontent show when she went into Malcolm's office. The only thing he hated more than whiners were salesmen, or so he said. And since local solicitors had long since learned their lesson about calling him—the hard way, but they'd learned it—she had no desire to be the low reporter on his totem pole. From what she'd seen in her time at the paper, bad things happened to those reporters…and she already had the crap assignments. She'd hate to see what would happen if she actually pissed off her boss.

It had taken her less than a minute to get to his office, but Malcolm was already engrossed in something else on the computer by the time she sat down in front of his desk. His distraction wasn't that unusual of an occurrence, so she settled in for a wait, patiently thumbing through her tablet as she did so. Seconds later, her phone buzzed with a text. Though she told herself not to get her hopes up, she couldn't stop herself from glancing at it, excitement welling up inside her at the possibility that it might be—

Nope. Not Nic. Just her friend and next-door neighbor, Serena, asking her to pick up some milk on the way home.

Her heart fell as she shoved the phone back in her pocket, despite the very stern talking-to that she gave herself. Of course it wasn't Nic. It hadn't been Nic in over three weeks. Which was fine. Better than fine. It was what she'd wanted, after all. Otherwise she would have answered one of the dozen text messages he'd sent her in the seven weeks since she'd snuck out of his house while he slept.

But she hadn't answered them, no matter what

approach he'd taken. Funny, sweet, friendly, sexy. She'd read them all—over and over again—but hadn't been able to bring herself to answer them. Not because she didn't like him, but because she did. Not because she thought he was a jerk, but because she thought he was kind of…sweet. And goofy. And far too charming for her own peace of mind.

As she'd looked at those text messages, she could see herself falling for him, and she couldn't afford to do that. Couldn't afford to open herself up to him only to find out she was wrong. She'd been hurt doing that too many times before to risk it now. Or ever again.

"So, Desi," her boss finally began. "I have a story for you to write."

"Excellent," she answered with as much enthusiasm as she could muster, even while inside she was rolling her eyes. She could only imagine what he wanted this time. Probably gossip coverage of some socialite's garden party or something equally ridiculous.

"You know, for someone who's been begging

to get out of the society pages for months, you certainly don't seem very excited about the opportunity."

It took a second for his words to sink in, but when they did she felt her whole body come to attention. Her gaze sharpened, her heart beat faster, and she leaned so far forward that she almost fell out of her chair. Even as she told herself to cool it—that she didn't even know what kind of story he was offering—her brain started racing with possibilities as excitement thrummed through her blood.

Malcolm must have seen the difference, because he laughed before saying, "Now there's the Desi I was expecting!" He nodded toward her tablet. "Ready to take notes?"

"Absolutely." If this was just some newly sadistic way for him to assign a high-society story to her, she swore she was going to kill him. And since she'd spent her off-hours moonlighting as the obituary writer for the past few months, she knew a bunch of ways to do it, too.

"So, I have a story for you. This morning, I got a tip about a business new to San Diego that might not be quite as legitimate as it seems on the surface."

Her mind started racing. Drugs. Guns. Mexican Mafia. She could practically feel herself champing at the bit to sink her teeth into whatever it was. She'd been trained in investigative journalism from a very early age by her father, one of the best reporters in the business. She could do this story. No, she *would* do this story.

"Diamonds," he told her after a brief pause that saw him turning back to his computer.

"Diamonds," she repeated. "Someone's using their business to smuggle diamonds?"

"I just sent the file I've begun assembling to your email," he told her as her tablet dinged to let her know she'd gotten mail. "It's got the basic information that the source gave me along with all of his contact info. I want you to get in touch with him, listen to his story the same way I did. Then I want you to do some digging. I want to know what's going on with this company, whether or not you think the accusations are true, and how you think it's happening."

"The diamond smuggling."

"I never said it was smuggling." He shot her a look. "Don't make assumptions. And look, I'm not just having you dig as an exercise. I really don't know if what this guy told me is true. If it is, it's a big damn deal. I just spent the last two hours researching these brothers, and if half of what this guy says turns out to be right, it's going to explode their whole damn lives. These guys have built their whole business on clean diamonds and—"

"Clean diamonds?" she asked, trying to wrap her head around the term. "Meaning not stolen?"

"*Clean* meaning responsibly sourced."

"Oh, of course. We're talking about conflict diamonds. Blood diamonds."

"Exactly."

"Bijoux." The name came to her easily, thanks to her time in the society pages. Much of San Diego's elite had been buzzing for the past few months about the fact that Marc Durand and his brother had come to town. They were big philanthropists and everyone wanted some of their money to support their pet charities—or themselves, for that matter.

She hadn't met either of the brothers yet. They'd been too busy setting up their business and their foundation to come to any of the galas she'd worked. Or if they had, she'd certainly never run into them. Which might be a good thing considering she was now going to be investigating them.

"Good," Malcolm told her with a satisfied nod.

"They're one of the biggest diamond corporations in the world right now, and you think they've been lying about where they get their diamonds."

"I don't know if they're lying or not, but your job is to figure out if they are. Right now, all I know is that somebody came to me and told me the brothers were pulling a fast one, masquerading as responsible diamond sourcers and then marking up the prices on conflict diamonds to ratchet up profits. I want to know if there's any truth to the story, and if there is, I want to know every single detail about it before we run this story and blow their whole business sky-high. You double-, triple- and quadruple-check this source and every other source you come across. Understand?"

"Absolutely." She opened up the file on her tablet, skimming over the information he'd sent her. Most of it was pretty sketchy, but she'd fix that soon enough. "When's the due date? And how many words do you want on this?"

Malcolm shook his head. "Let's just see how it goes. You find out if this is just some disgruntled ex-employee blowing smoke. If he is, the story goes away."

"And if he isn't?"

"If he isn't, we'll cross that bridge when we come to it. It will be a huge story and I'm thinking you'll probably need a partner to write it with you."

"I don't need a partner—" she started, but he held up a hand.

"Look, I know you're good. I know you're ready to show me what you've got. But you're still a rookie reporter and it doesn't matter how good you are, kid. There's no way I'm trusting a story this big to a snot-nosed society reporter."

"You're going to use me for the grunt work

and then cut me out." She kept her voice calm when all she really wanted to do was curse. This could be her big break, and he was already talking about taking it away from her.

"I didn't say that. What I said was that I'm going to let you investigate and if you get something, I'm going to let you help write the biggest story of your career to date. If you want to write this story, if you want to see your byline front page above the fold, you need to give me something to work with. Show me what you got."

"Of course." She nodded calmly while inside she was dancing. What he said made sense— and it was fair. She would investigate the hell out of this story, find out everything she could and even find out the angle she wanted to take. Maybe she'd even write the article and present it to him as a fait accompli. Then he would see what she could do and make an informed decision about how to proceed. And if she did this right—if she triple-checked her sources and dotted every i and crossed everything that even looked like a t—then he wouldn't have a choice.

He'd have to move her out of the society pages and into news. Or at least into features.

This was what she'd been waiting for. Her big break. The story she'd been dying to tell.

"Got it?" Malcolm asked again.

Oh, she had it. God, did she ever. "Got it," she agreed.

"Good. Then go do your job. And don't forget, this is an extra assignment. You've still got your society-page duties—including that party tomorrow night. I'll cut down on you some, so you've got time to work on this on the clock, but you can't let the rest of your stories suffer for it."

"I won't."

He nodded, looking satisfied. Then, out of nowhere, he gestured wildly toward the door. "So go! Does it look like I've got time to stand around here chatting all damn day?"

"Right. I'm going." She quickly picked up her stuff, headed toward the door. But she stopped right before she crossed the threshold, turning back to look at him. "Thanks for giving me a shot. I won't let you down."

"I know you won't, kid. I knew the second I

saw that picture that you would be perfect for the job."

"Picture?" she asked. "What picture?"

"The one of you and Nic Durand at the Children's Hospital Gala in San Diego a few weeks ago. It was in the files under Bijoux when I went to look. Pretty dress, by the way."

She felt all the blood drain from her face as his words sunk in. "Me and Nic *Durand*?"

"Yeah. You look surprised. Didn't you get his name before you danced with him?"

Oh, God. Oh, God. Ohgod! Panic hit her like a freight train as she figured out that Nic—*her* Nic—was actually Nic Durand. But that was impossible. He'd said he was a PR guy. She remembered every second of the time she spent with him and she remembered, very clearly, him saying he worked in public relations. Then again, maybe he hadn't.

Something like that.

Those were his exact words when she'd asked him what he did. She'd leaped to the conclusion that he was a PR guy and he'd let her make the leap. More, he'd encouraged her to do it.

Typical, she told herself as she tried to tamp down the fury and the fear rocketing through her. He hadn't wanted her to know who he really was, hadn't wanted her to know how much money he was worth, just in case she decided to try to sink her claws into him. As if she'd ever do something like that. As if she would ever even consider sinking her claws into any man.

But figuring all this out now didn't make her current situation any less precarious. What was she supposed to do? Obviously, this was a very clear conflict of interest. She'd *slept* with Nic Durand, for God's sake. And then blown him off. And now she was supposed to investigate him? Fairly and impartially and with a very definite eye on the prize of becoming a reporter who did real stories as opposed to one who covered whose designer dress was actually an imitation?

How could she do it? How could she not do it, when she was standing in the middle of Malcolm's office and he was looking at her so expectantly? Maybe even paternally. She didn't want to disappoint him, but she also didn't know if she could do this. Didn't know if she could investigate Nic and his brother for something so despicable when—up until two minutes ago—there'd been a part of her that had longed to see him again for very nonbusiness reasons.

She must have been standing there trying to figure things out for longer than she'd thought, because Malcolm suddenly put a bracing hand on her shoulders. "Everything okay there, Desi?" he asked gruffly.

"Yes, of course," she lied. "Sorry, I was just thinking about what angle to take with my investigation."

"Well, I'd start by using the gala angle."

She looked at him blankly. "The gala angle?"

"Sure. You've already met him at least once, right?"

"Yes."

"Then call him up. Ask him for a tour of his business. Tell him you're writing a story about Bijoux since they're new to the area and set to become a major power player in Southern California. Men like that enjoy having their egos stroked."

"You want me to lie to him?" Was it possible for her to feel any sicker about this whole situation?

Malcolm glared at her sternly. "You're an investigative reporter, Maddox. You use whatever contacts you have to find out the truth. That's the way the job works."

"I know that, sir. It's just that—"

"Just what? I gave you this story because I figured you already had an in with Nic Durand. Was I wrong about that? Should I give the story to someone else?"

He looked far from pleased at the prospect, and she knew if she followed her gut, if she told him yes he should give the story to someone else, he would do just that. And it would be a cold day in hell before she ever got another chance. She'd be writing obituaries and party gossip for as long as she worked for the *Los Angeles Times*. And maybe even longer.

"No, of course not," she told him, putting every ounce of conviction she could muster into her voice. Which wasn't much, if she was being honest, but at this point she would take what she could get.

"You don't sound too sure about that."

"I am sure. I've got this."

Malcolm finally nodded, satisfied. "Well, go get them, then. And don't forget to ask for help if you need it."

"I won't," she told him before making her way out of his office and back to her desk. As she did, her stomach pitched and rolled at the thought of the mess she had gotten herself into.

What was she supposed to do?

Then again, what could she do?

The questions echoed in her mind like a particularly terrifying mantra. But no matter how many times she asked them, no matter how many scenarios she ran through, she couldn't find a solution. She was going to have to investigate Nic Durand. And if he was guilty of what he was accused of...if he was guilty, she was going to have to write an article that exposed that guilt to the whole world.

The thought made her sick.

Because whatever his reasons for not telling

her who he was—and she was forced to admit his omission could have been for any number of reasons besides him thinking she was a gold digger—after all, she hadn't exactly told him what she did for a living, either, had she?—he didn't deserve her using their connection, or whatever it was, to trick him into letting her inside Bijoux.

She had never used her body to get what she wanted, and she'd be damned if she'd use it now, even after the fact. No, she decided as she sat at her desk scrolling through the folder Malcolm had emailed her. If she had to do this investigation, then she would do it *her* way. Without involving Nic until she had no other choice in the matter. And when she'd reached that point, when she'd gathered as much information as she could on his company's diamond procurement, she would go to him. But she would do it the right way. She would be totally honest about who she was and what she wanted.

It was the only way she could do it, as far as she could tell. The only way she could write the story and also keep her integrity. Anything else was out of the question.

Satisfied with her decision—or at least as satisfied as she could be—she skimmed through the rest of the file before pulling out a yellow legal pad and making a list of every question she could think of pertaining to the investigation. It was just a start. She was sure she would come up with a bunch more as she delved into her research. But she needed to start somewhere, and this seemed as good a way to focus her research as any other.

Always start with the questions, her father used to tell her. How do you know what you're looking for if you don't even know what information you're missing? He'd said that to her a million times when she was young, back when he actually used to come home from his sojourns on the road. Back when he—when they—still had a home for him to come back to.

Shoving the unpleasant memories away, she dug into the story just as he'd taught her all those years ago. And soon she was so engrossed in her research that she forgot about everything else. It turned out the diamond trade was a fascinating—and brutal—world, one where human lives were often valued much less than the stones they mined.

She was so riveted by the stories that she didn't even notice Stephanie stopping by her desk until her friend put her hand on Desi's arm. Then she nearly jumped through the roof.

"I'm sorry!" Stephanie laughed when Desi had finally calmed down enough to take a breath. "I just wanted to see if you were ready to go to lunch."

"Oh, yeah. Of course. Give me five minutes to get all this in order, if that's okay."

"No problem. Looks like you got a decent story after all."

"Looks like. I hope I can do it justice."

"Of course you can! You'll be off the galas and into the news pages in no time."

"From your mouth to God's ears," Desi told her.

"Hush! Don't let Malcolm hear you say that. He'll think you're talking about him!"

They both laughed then, largely because Stephanie was right.

Desi closed her computer and locked up all of

her paper research in her desk. It was early days yet, but it was never too early to be careful with her information. Another lesson her father had taught her before she'd hit her tenth birthday.

"Ready to go?" she asked after gathering her purse.

"Absolutely." But before she could step out from behind her desk, Stephanie leaned closer and whispered, "Actually, I was hoping you had a tampon I could borrow. I always carry a couple in my purse, but for some reason I only had one today and there's no way I'll make it through the afternoon without an extra."

"Oh, right. Of course. I keep mine in my desk." Desi turned to open the drawer where she kept her personal stuff and pulled out the box of tampons she'd put in there weeks ago. But as she opened the box, it hit her that it was *un*opened. As in it had *never* been opened.

But that was impossible. She'd brought the box to work eight or nine weeks ago, when she'd used up the last of the old one. How could she have not had a period in the past nine weeks? And, more important, how could she not have noticed? She'd never had the most regular periods, despite being on the pill, but she'd never gone this long without one before, either. Alarm bells should have sounded at one point or another. They were definitely sounding now.

"Are you okay?" Stephanie asked as she reached out a hand to steady Desi's suddenly shaky form. "You've gone pale."

Desi didn't answer. She was too busy doing the math in her head. And then redoing it. And then redoing it again. But no matter how she looked at it, no matter how she counted, she should have had a period before now. Even worse, if she'd been close to her regular schedule last month, she would have been ovulating right about the time she and Nic had met.

Her knees gave way at the realization, and she probably would have fallen if Stephanie hadn't shoved the desk chair under Desi at the last second.

"Are you okay?" her friend asked again.

"I don't know." The words sounded hoarse as she forced them out of her too-tight throat. It wasn't possible. It just wasn't possible. She had been on the pill for years. And except for that first time on the balcony, she and Nic had used condoms. Which shouldn't have mattered in terms of pregnancy because she was on. The. Pill.

Except...except, she hadn't had a period. And—she took stock of her body, which felt totally normal except for the low-grade dizziness she'd been fighting for a few days—she had none of the signs that she would soon be getting a period. No cramps. No aching. No spotting. Nothing.

Nothing but dizziness. Nothing but a missed period. Nothing but—oh, God. Ohgodohgodohgod. For a second she thought she was actually going to have to put her head between her legs.

"Can you tell me what's wrong?" Stephanie asked, crouching down beside her. "Are you sick?"

Desi laughed a little hysterically then. "No, I'm not sick." And she wasn't, though she was very afraid that she was going to get sick if she didn't stave off this dizziness. And since the last thing she wanted to do was throw up in the middle of her office, she started breathing in through her nose and out through her mouth in the same steady rhythm she'd once seen a pregnant professor use.

It actually worked and in less than a minute she was feeling a lot steadier. At least physically. "Um, maybe you should go to lunch without me," she told Stephanie as she thrust the whole box of tampons at her. All she could think of was getting to the nearest drugstore and buying a pregnancy test. It would come back negative— of course it would come back negative because she was on the pill—but she needed to see the minus sign. Or the blank box. Or whatever the hell it was she was supposed to see, or not see, to prove to herself that she wasn't pregnant with Nic Durand's baby.

Except something in her wildly erratic behavior must have given her away—could it have been her death grip on the box of unopened tampons?—because Stephanie hauled her gently to her feet. Then whispered softly, "The convenience store on the corner should have a pregnancy test. If you'd like, I can run and get it for you."

Desi should have said she was fine, that she appreciated the offer but she could get the pregnancy test herself. Or better yet, she should have pretended that she had no idea what Stephanie was talking about. But the truth was, she was suddenly exhausted and shaky and terrified. So terrified. The last thing she wanted to do at that moment was to walk down the street and buy a damn pregnancy test that might change the course of the rest of her life.

And so she said yes to Stephanie's very kind offer. And then, after fumbling a twenty out of her wallet, she sat at her desk as her friend took off for the street as fast as her four-inch heels could carry her.

Desi didn't know how long Stephanie was gone, but she knew she didn't move, didn't think, barely even breathed in the time between when her friend left and when she returned, a small brown paper bag in her hand. How could Desi move when it felt as if her whole life hung in the balance?

"Go do it now," Stephanie urged as she handed over the bag. "It's better to know than not know."

Desi agreed, which was how she found herself alone in a bathroom stall, peeing on a small white stick. According to the directions, there'd be one line no matter what—pregnant or not pregnant. But if she was pregnant...

Except, she didn't have to wait five minutes. She didn't even have to wait one. By the time she had pulled her pants back up, there were two purple lines. Two very distinct purple lines.

She was pregnant with Nic Durand's baby, and she didn't have a clue what she was supposed to do about it.

Six

"Nic, there's a reporter on line two for you," his secretary said from where she was standing in the doorway to his office. "A Darlene Bloomburg from the *Los Angeles Times.*"

He didn't bother glancing up from his laptop, where he was reviewing his marketing team's suggestions for Bijoux's winter ad campaigns. It was only July, but he wanted to ensure they made a huge splash with the holiday crowd. It was the next step in his plan to make Bijoux diamonds a household name. "Pass her over to Ollie," he suggested, referring to the head of Bijoux's public relations department. "She can get whatever she needs from him."

"I tried that," Katrina told him. "But she's determined to talk to you."

Something about the urgency in her voice snagged his attention, had him looking up from the proposed ad campaign and trying to figure out what he was missing. His secretary was a thirty-year veteran in her field, and totally unflappable most days, so the fact that she was standing in front of him, wringing her hands and biting her lip, didn't bode well for any of them.

"Is there something going on that I should know about?" he asked.

"I don't know. But I looked her up when she was so insistent, and she's the managing editor for the *Times*. Not the typical reporter we get calling us for a quote or some information on the diamond business."

"You think she's fact-checking an article about Bijoux?"

She nodded nervously. "I think she might be, yes."

"How come I didn't know the West Coast's largest paper was writing an article about us?"

"I don't know."

"Well, I'm going to find out. Tell the reporter—what's her name?"

"Darlene Bloomburg, sir."

"Tell Bloomburg that I'll be with her in a couple minutes. In the meantime, get Ollie in here, will you, please?"

"Right away, Nic."

Less than two minutes later, his PR director walked through the door, looking calm and collected despite the fact that he'd hightailed it over here from the other end of the floor.

"You know anything about this story?" Nic asked the other man.

Ollie shook his head. "No, nothing. But I'm sure it's nothing to worry about. Probably just a puff piece. We are in the middle of wedding season, after all."

"Maybe." But something felt off to Nic about that answer. Managing editors didn't usually need to fact-check fluff pieces. They had copy editors for stuff like that. "Let's just find out, shall we?" He reached for the phone and put it on speaker.

"This is Nic Durand."

"Hello, Mr. Durand. My name is Darlene Bloomburg and I'm managing editor of the *Los Angeles Times*."

"Please, call me Nic. It's nice to meet you, Darlene. What can I do for you?"

"I'm calling because we'll be running an article about Bijoux on the front page of Friday's edition and I wanted to check some facts as well as give you a chance to make a statement about the article's claims."

An alarm bell went off in his head and his eyes shot to Ollie, who looked as clueless as Nic felt. "You want me to make a statement."

"If you'd like to, yes."

"About what, may I ask?"

"About the fact that the *Times* has uncovered some credible information that proves Bijoux has been passing off conflict diamonds as conflict-free ones for several years."

The single alarm bell turned into a full-fledged five-alarm brigade. "That's impossible," he said. "What's your source?" Beside him, Ollie started turning red and making a stop gesture with his hands. Nic ignored him as the top of his own head threatened to blow off.

"What's impossible? That we've uncovered the evidence or—"

"That you think you can prove such a thing when it is blatantly untrue. I'm going to ask you again. What's your source?"

"It's the policy of the *Times* to never reveal a source. Am I correct in understanding that you dispute our findings, then?"

"Damn right I dispute them. Bijoux deals only in conflict-free diamonds and has for the ten years that Marc Durand and I have been in charge of this company. And it's Bijoux's policy to sue anyone who commits libel by printing otherwise."

"I see. Do you have any proof to back up your claims that your diamonds are conflict-free?"

"Are you serious with this? You're the one accusing me of lying and cheating and, more importantly, of buying diamonds from countries that allow the enslavement and murder of children as long as it results in gems for them to sell.

I feel like you're the one who needs to provide the proof in this situation."

Next to him, Ollie changed from red to a very unbecoming shade of purple even as he waved his arms as if he was trying to attract the attention of a rescue plane. More to prevent his top PR guy from having a stroke in the middle of what promised to be the mother of all PR crises than because Nic wanted his help at that moment, Nic hit Mute on the phone and then asked, "What do you want me to say?"

"I want you to get the article," Ollie demanded. "There's no way they run that article without you seeing it first. Tell her—"

"I know what to tell her. You go get Hollister." He wanted Bijoux's head counsel in here, stat.

Nic unmuted the phone, this time hitting the button so hard that the entire device skidded a foot across his desk. Son of a bitch. He was going to get that article and then he was going to tear it—and the reporter who wrote it—apart with his bare hands. "I need to tell you, Darlene, that if you run that article as is, without giving me a chance to vet it first and debunk your ob-

vious misinformation, you will be facing a law-
suit the likes of which the *Los Angeles Times*
has never seen."

"Our information is good."

"Your information is wrong, that much I guarantee you."

"It comes from an insider at Bijoux. One who
has proof that the company has systematically
bought conflict diamonds and passed them off
as conflict-free diamonds for at least seven of
the last ten years."

"Let me get this straight. You're claiming that
one of my people came to you and gave you
information implicating us in not only buying
conflict diamonds but then in conspiring to de-
fraud consumers by claiming the gems are conflict-free."

"Essentially, yes, that is what the source has
provided us proof of."

"And again, this came from one of our people?"

"That is correct."

"And you think you're going to run this article
in three days."

"We *are* going to run this article in three days,"

Over his dead body they were. "Yeah, well, Darlene, that just isn't going to happen."

"With all due respect, Nic—"

"With all due respect, Darlene, you've been taken for a ride."

"The *Los Angeles Times* does not get taken for a ride, Mr. Durand. We triple-check our sources—"

"Well, you didn't in this case. This is the first time either Marc or myself has heard of these allegations, and in a situation like this, no one else is in a position to know more about our diamonds, and where they come from, than we do. I know where every single shipment comes from. Marc personally inspects every mine on a regular basis. The certification numbers on the stones come straight to us, and only our in-house diamond experts ever get near those numbers. All of our diamonds are conflict-free. All of them. Now, you are welcome to come in and tour our facilities and see all of the safeguards we have in place to ensure that what you're accusing us of doesn't happen. In the meantime,

I'll be happy to courier over all of our PR materials so you can see where our diamonds really do come from."

"Our reporter tried to come for a tour on two separate occasions while she was researching this article. Both times she was turned away by your PR office."

He ground his teeth together, wondering what the hell Ollie had been thinking. Probably that he didn't have time to babysit a reporter on a puff piece, what with the sudden uptick in business and philanthropy—and the publicity both generated. But if she had told him what the story was about, there was no way Ollie would have turned her away. And no way this information wouldn't have been brought to Nic's attention a hell of a lot sooner than three days before the article was supposed to run.

Which, he figured, was exactly why the reporter hadn't told anyone the nature of the story she was writing. And now they were all paying for it…

"Your reporter's inability to explain her article idea to my PR department is not my fault."

"Of course not. But your PR department's secrecy and inability to deal with the community when necessary is not our fault, either."

He ground his teeth, counted to ten to keep from spewing onto her all the vitriol that was racing through his brain. When he could finally speak again without fear of telling the managing editor of the *Los Angeles Times* to go to hell and take her newspaper with her, he said, "I'll courier over that information to you right away. In the meantime, you can email or fax a copy of that article to my office."

"We are under no obligation to do so, Mr. Durand." Her voice was firm, with absolutely no uncertainty whatsoever. Which seemed impossible to him considering the claims she was making—and the proof he had to refute them.

Who was her source? he wondered again. He went through a list of all the employees who had left recently and couldn't think of one who would do this—or who *could* do this. All of them had left on good terms, and not one of them had access to the kind of information that would convince the *Times* to run such a negative story. Largely because that information didn't exist, but still. If it did, no way any of them would have been able to access it.

"You may not be under any obligation, Darlene, but you're going to do it anyway. Because if you don't, my attorneys will be filing for injunctions today against your paper, you and the reporter who wrote this drivel. And if you run this article as is, without getting to the truth of the matter, I will sue you. By the time we're done, Bijoux will own the *Los Angeles Times* and all of your assets. Now, you have until eleven o'clock to provide me with a copy of that article. Or the Los Angeles civil court system will be hearing from us."

He hung up the phone without giving her the chance to say another word. He'd heard more than enough.

For long seconds, Nic could do nothing but stand there, staring into space and imagining the worst-case scenario if this thing went to print. Bijoux would lose everything it had gained under Marc and Nic's leadership. They'd be crucified in the press—and in the international human rights community. They'd be sued by God only knew how many consumer groups and diamond retailers. And they'd be investigated by numerous federal and international law agencies. Not to mention the fact that if any of that happened, it would break his brother's heart.

Which was why Nic was going to make sure that it didn't. He and Marc had worked too hard to build up this company after they'd taken it over ten years before. They'd faced their father's disapproval, their board's disapproval. Hell, even the industry had frowned on Marc and Nic's determination to use only responsibly sourced diamonds.

In the interim years, the industry had grown much more supportive of what he and his brother were doing—largely because of the growing interest from human rights groups in places like Sierra Leone and Liberia. New laws had been passed making trading in conflict diamonds illegal, but just because it was illegal didn't mean that less reputable companies didn't still buy up conflict diamonds. It only meant they did it in secret instead of on the open market as they used to.

He and Marc did not do that. They did not buy conflict diamonds. They didn't work with anyone who dealt in conflict diamonds. And they sure as hell didn't cover up their illegal activity by passing the diamonds off to consumers at a jacked-up price.

The accusation was absurd, completely and totally ludicrous. But that didn't matter. Once it was out there, once the general public got hold of it, Bijoux's brand would be annihilated and everything he and Marc had worked so hard for would be destroyed right along with it.

There was no way he would let that happen. Not to his brother, not to his employees and not to the family business he'd worked so many long, hard hours to develop. If the *Los Angeles Times* really wanted to pick a fight with him, then it'd better come at him with everything it had. Because he was about to make it his life's mission to bring those bastards down.

"We have a problem."

His brother looked up as Nic blew right past

Marc's assistant and entered his office with a slam of his door.

"What's going on?" Marc asked, looking faintly alarmed.

Operating on instinct, and rage, Nic slammed his hand down on the desk hard enough to rattle everything resting on top of it—including Marc's laptop and cup of coffee. Then watched as his brother grabbed the coffee and put it on the credenza behind him despite the obvious tension in the air. Such a Marc thing to do. Staying calm when Nic was still so furious he could barely think, let alone form coherent sentences.

When he turned back to face Nic, Marc was completely composed, but he figured that wasn't going to last long. His brother might be the cool one of the two of them, but he was even more ragingly protective of this business than Nic was. Once he heard what was going on, Marc would lose it as completely as Nic had.

"Tell me."

"I just got off the phone with a reporter from the *Los Angeles Times*. She's doing an exposé on Bijoux and wanted a comment before the article goes to print."

"An exposé? What the hell does she have to expose?" Marc stood up then and walked around the desk. "Between you and me, we're in charge of every aspect of this company. Nothing happens here that we don't know about, and we run a clean company."

"That's exactly what I told her." Nic shoved a hand through his hair as he tried to make sense of the situation for what felt like the millionth time. They were good to their employees, treated them well. Gave them raises twice a year, bonuses once a year. Hell, they'd built a state-of-the-art facility on the edge of the ocean, one that provided everything from free health care to free day care and three meals a day for their employees.

He and Marc were invited to weddings, christenings, birthday parties…and they went, every time. Fostering a sense of community, of family, within the company was incredibly important to him—probably because he'd never had much of a family beyond his brother. The fact that someone would be so disgruntled, so angry, *so vengeful*, that the person would deliberately sabotage them like this…it made absolutely no sense.

"And?" Marc ground out the words. "What's she exposing?"

God, Nic didn't want to tell his brother this. Didn't want to see how devastated he was going to be at the accusation. Not when Marc had poured his heart and soul into making Bijoux not only a success, but also a company with a heart and a social conscience.

Still, it had to be done, and Nic might as well rip the bandage off as quickly, as cleanly as possible. "According to her, she's exposing the fact that we're pulling diamonds from conflict areas, certifying them as conflict-free and then passing them on to the consumer at the higher rate to maximize profits."

Marc's mouth actually dropped open, and for long seconds he did nothing but stare at Nic. "That's ridiculous," he finally sputtered.

"I know it's ridiculous! I told her as much. She

says she has an unimpeachable source who has given her credible evidence."

"Who's the source?"

"She wouldn't tell me that." Nic fought the urge to slam his hand into the wall as frustration welled up in him all over again.

"Of course she wouldn't tell you that, because the source is bullshit. The whole story is bullshit. I know where every single shipment of diamonds comes from. I personally inspect every mine on a regular basis. The certification numbers come straight to me, and only our in-house diamond experts—experts whom I have handpicked and trust implicitly—ever get near those numbers."

"I told her *all* of that. I invited her to come in and take a tour of our new facilities and see exactly how things work here at Bijoux."

"And what did she say?"

"She said she had tried to come for a tour, but PR had put her off. It's too late now. The story is slotted to run on Friday, and they really want a comment from us before it goes to print."

"Friday's in three days."

"I'm aware of that. It's why I'm here, freaking out."

"Screw that." Marc picked up his phone and dialed an in-house number. They both waited impatiently for the line to be picked up.

"Hollister Banks." The voice of their lead counsel came through the speakerphone. He was obviously out of his earlier meeting—and just as obviously hadn't yet gotten the urgent message Nic had left for him. He sounded far too cheerful.

"Hollister. This is Marc. I need you in my office now."

"Be there in five."

His brother didn't bother to say goodbye before hanging up and dialing another number. "Lisa Brown, how may I help you?"

Nic listened as Marc told their top diamond inspector the same thing he'd just told Hollister.

"But, Marc, I just got in a whole new shipment—"

"So put it in the vault and then get up here." The impatience in his voice must have gotten through to her, because Lisa didn't argue again. She agreed before quietly hanging up the phone.

It took Lisa and Hollister only a couple of minutes to get to Marc's office, and soon the four of them were gathered in the small sitting area to the left of his desk. No one said a word as Nic once again recounted his discussion with Darlene Bloomburg.

He got angrier and angrier as he told the story. By the end, he was literally shaking with rage. This was more than just his company they were screwing. It was his life, his brother's life, his employees' lives. If Bijoux went down for this—and he'd been in marketing long enough to know that if this story ran, they would absolutely take major hits no matter how untrue the accusations were—it'd be more than just Marc's and Nic's asses on the line. His employees would be under investigation and, if the hits were bad enough, also out of jobs. All because some ignorant reporter with a chip on her shoulder couldn't get her facts straight.

As he tried to channel his rage, he promised himself that if this story ran he would make it his life's mission to get that reporter fired. Hell, he'd get her fired even if it didn't run. She should have known better than to make this kind of mistake.

"Who's the source?" Marc asked Lisa after she and Hollister had absorbed the story—and its implications.

"Why are you asking me? I have no idea who would make up a false claim like this and feed it to the *Times*. I'm sure it's none of our people."

"The reporter seemed pretty adamant that it was an insider. Someone who had the position and the access to prove what he or she is saying." It was the third time Nic had said those words, and they still felt disgusting in his mouth.

"But that's impossible. Because what the person is saying isn't *true*. The claims are preposterous," Lisa asserted. "Marc and I are the first and last in the chain of command when it comes to accepting and certifying the conflict-free diamonds. There's no way one of us would make a mistake like that—and we sure as hell wouldn't lie about the gems being conflict-free to make extra money. So even if someone messed with the diamonds between when I see them and when Marc does, he would catch it."

"Not to mention the fact that there are cameras everywhere, manned twenty-four/seven by security guards who get paid very well to make sure no one tampers with our stones." Everyone in the room knew that already, but Nic felt the need to add it anyway.

"What this person is saying just isn't possible," Lisa continued. "That's why Marc insists on being the last point of contact for the stones before we ship them out. He verifies the geology and the ID numbers associated with them."

"There is a way it would work," Marc interrupted, his voice a little weaker than usual. "If I were involved in the duplicity, it would explain everything."

"But you're not!" Nic said at the same time Lisa exclaimed, "That's absurd!"

Nic knew his brother almost as well as he knew himself, and if there was one thing he was certain of it was that Marc would never do anything to harm Bijoux. The two of them had worked too hard to get the company to where it was to let a little extra profit ruin everything. They already had more money than they could spend in three lifetimes. Why risk it all, especially in such a despicable way, for some extra cash?

People *died* mining conflict diamonds. Children were exploited, beaten, starved, worked nearly to death. No amount of extra profit was worth propagating such blatant human rights violations. No amount of money was worth the stain dealing in conflict diamonds would leave on his soul.

"Marc's making sense. It's what they'll argue," Hollister said, and though it was obvious by his tone that he disagreed, Nic could tell his ready agreement bothered Marc.

Not that Nic blamed Hollister. This was more than a company to them, more than profits and bottom lines. More even than diamonds. Their great-grandfather had started Bijoux in the early twentieth century and it had been run by a Durand ever since.

When Nic and Marc took it over, they'd had to act fast to repair the damage their father had done through years of neglect and disinterest. It wasn't that he'd wanted to run the company into the ground, but he'd always been more interested in the adventures—and the women—the Durand money could buy rather than the day-to-day work of being CEO.

Which was why Nic and his brother had worked so hard to rebuild things. For years, they'd put their lives into this company and in a decade had managed to take Bijoux from a floundering behemoth into the second-largest diamond distributor in the world. They'd brought it into the twenty-first century and had created a business model that would help those who couldn't help themselves and that wouldn't exploit those who needed protection most.

"I don't care what you have to do," Marc told Hollister after a long pause. "I want that story stopped. We've worked too hard to build this company into what it is to have another setback—especially one like this. The jewel theft six years ago hurt our reputation and nearly bankrupted us. This will destroy everything Nic and I have been trying to do. You know as well as I do, even if we prove the accusations false in court, the stigma will still be attached. Even if we get the *Los Angeles Times* to print a retraction, it won't matter. The damage will have already been done. I'm not having it. Not this time. Not about something like this."

His words echoed Nic's thoughts from earlier, and the similarity was eerie enough to make the situation really sink in. From the moment he'd heard about the article, he'd been operating under the assumption that they would find a way to stop it. But what if they didn't? What if it actually got printed? What if everything they'd worked so hard for actually went up in smoke?

What would they do then?

What would *he* do then?

Marc must have been thinking along the same lines, because there was a renewed urgency in his voice when he told Hollister, "Call the editor. Tell him the story is blatant bullshit and if he runs it I will sue their asses and tie them up in court for years to come. By the time I'm done, they won't have a computer to their name let alone a press to run the paper on."

"I'll do my best, but—"

"Do better than your best. Do whatever it takes to make it happen. If you have to, remind them that they can't afford to go against Bijoux in today's precarious print-media market. If they think they're going to do billions of dollars of damage to this company with a blatantly false story based on a source they won't reveal, and that I won't retaliate, then they are bigger fools than I'm already giving them credit for. You can assure them that if they don't provide me with definitive proof as to the truth of their claims, then I will make it my life's work to destroy everyone and everything involved in this story. And when you tell them that, make sure they understand I don't make idle threats."

"I'll lay it out for them. But Marc," Hollister cautioned, "if you're wrong and you've antagonized the largest newspaper on the West Coast—"

"I'm not wrong. We don't deal in blood diamonds. We will *never* deal in blood diamonds, and anyone who says differently is a damn liar."

"I already made those threats to the managing

editor," Nic said after everyone absorbed Marc's words. "And while I agree they'll sound better coming from our lead counsel, we need to do more than threaten them. We need to prove to them that they're wrong."

"And how exactly are we going to do that?" Lisa asked. "If we don't know who they're getting information from, or even what that information is, how can we contradict them?"

"By hiring an expert in conflict diamonds." Hollister had obviously gotten with the program. "By taking him up to Canada where we get our stock, letting him examine the mines we pull from. And then bringing him back here and giving him access to anything and everything he wants. We don't have any secrets—at least not of the blood-diamond variety. So let's prove that."

"Yes, but getting an expert of that caliber on board could take weeks," Lisa protested. "There are barely a dozen people in the world with the credentials to sign off unquestioningly on our diamonds. Even if we pay twice the going rate, there's no guarantee that one of them will be available."

"But one is available." Nic glanced at his brother when he said it, knowing very well that Marc would not appreciate his suggestion. But desperate times called for desperate measures, and he would do anything—anything—to stop this from happening. Including dig up his brother's very painful past. "She lives right here in San Diego and teaches at GIA. She could totally do it."

Marc knew whom Nic was talking about, and he didn't take the suggestion well. Big shock there. Nic waited for him to say something, but when Marc did nothing but stand there silently, Nic couldn't help goading him. "Dude, you look like you swallowed a bug."

"I can't call Isa, Nic. She'd laugh in my face. Or she'd deliberately sabotage us just to get back at me. There's no way I can ask her to do this."

Nic rolled his eyes. "Weren't you the one saying we can't afford to screw around with this? Isa's here, she has the experience, and if you pay her well and get a sub to carry her classes, she's probably available. It doesn't get much better than that."

"You should give her a call," Hollister urged.

"Yeah, absolutely," agreed Lisa. "I'd forgotten about Isabella Moreno being here in San Diego. I've met her a few times and she's really lovely— we should totally get her. I can try to talk to her, if you'd like."

"No," Marc told Lisa harshly, after a few uncomfortable seconds passed. "I'll take care of getting her on board."

He didn't sound happy about it, but he looked resigned. And wary. Which was good enough for Nic. His brother was an arrogant bastard, but Bijoux meant everything to him. He'd get Isa on board, even if it meant he had to crawl to do it.

In the meantime, Nic would meet with Ollie and scour the article that should be in his inbox by now. If the worst case happened and this thing actually went to print, he wanted to be ready with the best damage control the industry had ever seen.

Seven

The next few days were excruciatingly slow as Nic waited for Isa's findings. He was sure Marc felt the same torture, but at least his brother was out in the world, actively working to save their company. He'd taken Isabella to Canada and now he was here, in the building with her, checking out their diamonds. Proving, unequivocally, once and for all, that whoever had given the *Times* its information had been wrong. All Nic was doing was sitting here, feeling as if he was fighting with both hands tied behind his back.

It wasn't a good feeling.

But then, how could it be when everything

he'd worked for, everything Marc had worked for, could go up in smoke any minute? Simply because someone with a grudge had lied about them. Simply because some reporter had said so. It was infuriating.

Nic and Ollie had put together a damn good plan for damage control over the past seventy-two hours, but Nic really hoped they'd never have to use it. Hollister had managed to get the article pushed back a few days, though not canceled, and now the only thing left to do was wait.

Wait for Isa to certify their diamonds as conflict-free.

Wait for the *Times* to decide what it would do about the article.

Wait for security to comb through the company files and find out the identity of the source.

Too bad he hated waiting with the passion of a thousand burning suns.

Yet, it seemed as if it was all he'd been doing lately. Even before this whole thing started. Ever since Nic had met Desi, really. He'd texted her a few times right after they'd been together, but she'd never responded. He'd dropped down to once a week after that because he hadn't wanted to harass her. He'd just wanted…her. If he hadn't, he would have given up after the second day.

But he hadn't given up. Instead, he'd waited seven weeks for her to respond to him and she never had. Not one returned text, not one phone call, nothing but total and complete radio silence. Which was why he'd finally given up on her, why he'd gone so far as to erase her number from his phone. He liked her a lot, but if she didn't feel the same way about him, he wasn't going to spend the next year moping around about the one who'd gotten away. Not when they'd spent less than twelve hours together total.

He'd thought if he shoved Desi out of his mind—and took her off his phone—he wouldn't have to think about her again.

Too bad it hadn't worked.

Determined to get her out of his mind once and for all, he grabbed his laptop. Started fiddling with the winter marketing plans. He'd had a great idea about them when he'd been wandering his empty house at three that morning. He should probably write it down before it disappeared.

But he'd only just opened the advertising budget spreadsheet when the intercom on his desk buzzed with his brother's voice. The sound cut through Nic's not-so-pleasant thoughts, giving him the distraction he'd been looking for. "Come to my office, will you? I want to talk to you about something."

"Be right there," Nic answered, glad beyond measure that he finally had something to do. Sure, he had his normal workload, but none of that interested him right now. Nothing did, except putting this story to rest once and for all.

Grabbing his phone and his cup of coffee off his desk, he made his way to Marc's office. As Nic walked down the long corridor that separated their corner offices, people called out hellos from every door that he passed.

He returned the greetings as naturally as he could, but he could tell his staff knew something was wrong. There were a bunch of questioning looks, and even their greetings were more subdued than normal. Not that he blamed them. He hadn't exactly been his normal exuberant self lately, either. It was pretty hard to act as if everything was all right when he and his brother might very well be captaining a sinking ship. They'd already been hit by the iceberg. Now they just had to wait to see if they'd somehow manage to stay afloat.

"What's up?" he asked as he let himself into Marc's office.

"I want to talk about the December ad campaign. I want to hit it harder, want to make sure we're everywhere we need to be."

"We will be, I promise."

"Still, I want to put more money toward the campaign. Another fifty million or so—"

"We don't need another fifty million—"

"You don't know that. You don't know what we'll need if—"

"I do know. And that's why we're retooling part of the campaign. There will still be the ads that focus on giving her diamonds, etc. But we'll also have ads about making the world a better place, bringing holiday cheer to those who have none—it'll have Bijoux's name on it, but there will be no mention of buying anything, no mention of gifts. Instead we'll focus on children in developing nations, with a particular emphasis on conflict diamonds and those who are forced to mine them."

"That's really smart, actually. I'm impressed."

"Don't sound so surprised. I do, occasionally, know what I'm doing, you know."

Marc snorted. "Well, let's not get all crazy now."

"Yeah, 'cause I'm the crazy one in the room."

"Excuse me? I will have you know that I am exceptionally sane."

"Yeah, that's what they all say, bro, right before they chop off an ear. Or some other more important body part."

"I assure you," Marc told him, completely deadpan, "I have no intention of chopping off *my* ear or anyone else's."

"Hey, don't knock it till you've tried it. Insanity might look good on you."

"But it already looks so good on you."

"I think you're confused. This isn't insanity, man. This is confidence."

Marc studied him for a second before shaking his head. "Nah. It's insanity."

Nic couldn't help it. He burst out laughing. It felt good to share a little banter with his brother, especially when things had been so tense lately. As he sank into a chair on the visitor's side of his brother's desk, he told himself it was a sign that things were looking up.

Harrison, one of the attorneys working their end of the situation and one of his closest friends at the company, walked in a couple of minutes later. He'd barely sat down before the door opened again and this time it was Isa who walked in, carrying a thick manila folder in her hand.

She grinned at all of them before perching on the corner of Marc's desk and sliding the folder across the dark cherrywood.

Mark looked at her inquisitively, at least until he opened it and saw what was written there. Then he broke out in a huge smile as he asked, "We got it?"

"You absolutely got it," Isa told him. "I didn't find one irregularity."

Adrenaline raced through Nic at the confirmation and he jumped out of his chair, pumped a fist in the air. "I knew it, baby!" he all but shouted. "I knew that reporter had a bad source." He gave Marc a second to look over the documentation she'd provided, then ripped the folder out of his hands and headed for the door.

"Hey, where are you going?" his brother called after him.

"To make a copy of this file. And then I'm going to go down to the *Los Angeles Times* myself and force-feed every single page of this to that jackal of a reporter. I hope she chokes on it."

"I feel obliged to warn you of the illegality of such actions." Harrison somehow managed to keep a straight face as he said it.

Nic flipped him off on his way out of the office. And though he wanted to celebrate with Marc and Isa and everyone else who had helped clear Bijoux of any wrongdoing, his job wasn't done yet. He needed to make sure the *Los Angeles Times*—and one particular reporter—got this information. And while he could, and would, have it emailed over, there was no way he was leaving this to the whims of someone's email habits. He was hand delivering this baby himself.

Besides, he really wanted to see D. E. Maddox's face when he plopped the report on her desk.

Since it was midmorning, the drive from their offices in north Carlsbad to the headquarters of the *Los Angeles Times* was less than an hour and a half. On the way, he plotted what he would say to Maddox and her managing editor. About a million expletives came to mind, but since he was a gentleman and not in the habit of cursing at women—even women who had nearly destroyed his family's business—he worked out a little speech instead. Short, pithy, to the point and—yes, he admitted it—more than a little smug. He might be a gentleman, but that didn't mean he shouldn't gloat a little. Especially about something like this.

He pulled into the parking lot exactly one hour and fourteen minutes after he left his office in Carlsbad—okay, maybe he'd sped a little, but he'd be lying if he said he wasn't anxious to get this whole thing over with and behind him. Behind Bijoux.

He figured he'd have to talk his way around a few security guards, maybe a receptionist or two, before he'd be able to get to either Maddox or Bloomburg. But it turned out that the huge compound that had once belonged exclusively to the *Los Angeles Times* now housed some kind of call center and a few other businesses that had nothing to do with the news. Which meant Nic waltzed right through the central lobby, where he checked the building's directory and got onto an elevator that took him straight to the newspaper's main floor.

He stepped off the elevator into a huge newsroom packed with desks. It was almost empty, which wasn't a surprise considering he'd arrived in the middle of the lunch hour. Except for a couple of stragglers, the few people who were there were huddled around a table at the front of the room, talking animatedly—probably about how to ruin the reputations of other businesses in the area. Which, okay, might be an unfair assessment, but he wasn't exactly feeling kindly toward the paper at the moment, or anyone who worked there.

There was still no receptionist to check in with, nobody to even give his name to. And while he knew security at Bijoux was over the top because of the nature of their business—and because they housed diamonds in their state-of-the-art vault—he admitted to being a little shocked at just how laissez-faire this place was about security.

Still, it worked in his favor, so he wasn't complaining. The paper had certainly had the element of surprise when it had contacted him less than a week ago. Now he was returning the favor. Neither Maddox nor Bloomburg would ever expect him to show up here. He'd find Maddox's desk and be waiting for her when she got back from lunch.

A big guy with a camera hanging around his neck finally stopped him when he was halfway through the room. But when Nic told him he had something to deliver to D. E. Maddox, the guy waved him toward a desk in the back corner. It was, surprisingly, one of only three desks in the cavernous space that actually had someone sitting at it.

Which was even more perfect. He'd prefer to confront Maddox and get this over with as quickly as possible.

As he approached, she had her back to him, which gave him a perfect view of what looked like miles of platinum blond hair. The sight tugged something inside of him, making him think of Desi and the night he'd spent with her hair fanned out on his pillow. He shoved the memory down—the last thing he needed right now was to be distracted by thoughts of her—but for some reason she just wouldn't leave his head. It was only when he got closer to the woman that he understood why that was.

As he approached her at an angle, he could see her profile clearly. Could see her high cheekbones and lush full lips. Could see her sun-kissed skin and the dimple low on her right cheek. Suddenly it didn't seem so far-fetched that she reminded him of the woman he had spent the past eighteen weeks trying to forget.

"Desi?" He hadn't meant to say her name out

loud, hadn't meant to attract her attention until he'd had a second to deal with the shock of finding out that D. E. Maddox, hated reporter and company annihilator, was none other than the woman he'd taken home for one unforgettable night.

But she turned toward him as soon as he said her name, her eyes widening as she realized who it was standing only a few feet from her desk. He expected her to look guilty, or at the very least, apologetic. Instead, her eyes burned with a fury that made the anger in his own gut look like nothing.

"What are you doing here?" she demanded as she pushed to her feet. "Slumming it?"

Slumming it? He couldn't even figure out what she meant, let alone how he was supposed to respond to the bizarre accusation. How could he understand when he was still reeling from the realization that *Desi* had been investigating him for weeks? That she'd been right under his nose for the past few days and he hadn't had a clue?

"Well?" she asked, and it was the impatience

in her voice that finally kick-started his brain into gear.

"I'm here to deliver this to D. E. Maddox," he said, brandishing the folder like the weapon it was. "But I have to admit I'm a little surprised to see *you* sitting at *her* desk."

"I don't know why you would be." She had the audacity to shrug. "It's not like you know anything about me."

"So you're really going to do this?" he demanded as the fury inside him kindled into ugly rage. "Pretend that nothing happened between us."

"Nothing did happen between us," she answered coolly. "At least, nothing important."

"So that night was what? A setup for this, then? A way for you to get to know your assignment before you ruined his business and his life?"

"I didn't ruin your life or your business. You did that all on your own when you decided to trade in conflict diamonds."

"I told your managing editor the other day and now I'm telling you. Bijoux does not deal in conflict diamonds." He dropped the folder on her desk. "I've got the proof that we don't right here."

She didn't even bother to glance down at the file. "And I have proof that you do."

"So show it to me."

"I'm not going to do that."

"Of course not. Who cares if you run a fake story as long as you get the attention you need, right?"

"I don't fake evidence," she said as she stood up and started around the desk. "And I didn't fake this story."

"Well, someone sure as hell faked evidence. Maybe it wasn't you. Maybe you're not inherently dishonest. Maybe you're just a sloppy reporter."

"Who do you think you are?" she demanded as she went toe-to-toe with him.

For a second—just a second—he was distracted by her flashing eyes and flushed skin. By her honeysuckle-and-vanilla scent. By her warmth. But then her words sank in and he found his temper flashing from dangerous to boiling point in the space of one breath and the next.

"Who do I *think* I am?" he repeated. "I don't think anything, sweetheart. I know exactly who I am. I'm the man whose career—and hundred-year-old family business—you set out to ruin on a whim. I'm the man you have accused of the vilest crimes and human rights violations imaginable. I'm the man you slept with to get a story and then dropped the moment you realized I wouldn't be useful to you."

"I didn't accuse you of anything you haven't done. And I didn't drop you. You dropped me."

He stared at her, speechless. For a moment, he honestly feared his head would explode. "Is that how you do it?" he wondered aloud. "Is that how you justify the lives you ruin? You just rewrite history to fit whatever version you need it to fit? You need a big story to break your career wide open? No problem. It's easy to manufacture evidence. You want to forget that you slept with me to get a story? That's easy. Just pretend I didn't text you for weeks trying to get you to talk to me." He threw his arms wide. "You've missed your calling, Desi. Oops, I mean D.E. You shouldn't be a journalist. You should be a

fiction writer. You'd probably top the charts with
your very first book."

She didn't answer him for long seconds. Instead she just stared at him with her jaw locked
and her eyes as cold and blue as the Pacific in
the middle of a midwinter temper tantrum.

"You don't know what you're talking about,"
she finally said.

"You know, you're going to call me a liar one
time too many and then…"

"And then what?"

He was too stunned by her brazenness and her
sheer lack of remorse to answer.

"That's what I thought," she sneered. "You've
got nothing."

Rage exploded within him, mixed with dis-
belief and confusion and more attraction than
he wanted to admit to, and Nic finally snapped.
Taking a step forward, he crowded her against
her desk before closing the last inches between
them. But the second his body brushed against
hers, he knew he'd made a mistake. Because
with that first touch, the low-grade attraction
that had hummed between them from the mo-

ment he'd said her name exploded into a conflagration of fiery want and desperate need.

He wasn't the only one affected. He could see Desi's awareness in her flushed skin. Could hear it in her ragged breathing and feel it in the not-quite-steady hands she pressed against his chest.

"What are you doing?" she whispered as he pressed even closer.

"I don't have a clue," he admitted.

"Then maybe you should stop."

"Maybe I should. But if you want me to do that, you probably shouldn't hold me quite so tightly." He glanced down to where she had tangled her fingers in his dress shirt.

She gasped then, started to pull back. But he didn't let her. Instead, he held her in place with one hand on her hip and the other between her shoulder blades.

Time stopped as they stood there, bodies locked together in a too-intimate bid for dominance—of the situation and each other. He didn't know what he was doing, didn't know what he was pushing for. All he knew was that part of him wanted to punish her for what she'd put him through but the other part of him wanted nothing more than to take her back to his house and make love to her until she screamed his name. Until she couldn't even think of defying him again.

They might have stayed there forever in their oddly intimate standoff, except just as Nic shifted to make sure she was comfortable, he felt a small but very definite kick against his abdomen.

"What was that?" he demanded, jumping back.

"That," she said, looking pointedly down at her gently rounded stomach, "is why I left you a voice mail."

Eight

She couldn't tell if Nic looked more stupefied or stupid as he gazed down at the firm curve of her stomach. "Close your mouth," she told him after a minute, "or you'll end up catching flies."

"You're pregnant?"

"Sure looks like it, doesn't it?" She didn't mean to be flippant, but come on. How long was he going to keep up this charade? After trying to get him on the phone three different times, she'd finally given up and broken the news to him in a voice mail. And she hadn't been delicate about the information, either. She'd told him, straight up, that she was pregnant and that she'd very much like it if he'd call her back.

Needless to say, he hadn't.

And now, here he was, looking completely shocked by her baby bump seconds after he'd accused her of falsifying evidence for her article. Which was total and complete bull. She'd double-, triple- and quadruple-checked everything in that article, so for him to come around here beating his chest and threatening her just because he didn't like what she'd found out… well, that wasn't exactly her problem, was it?

Except the longer he stood there, the more it began to feel as if it was totally her problem. And when the elevators started dinging, marking the return of most of the staff, she knew she had to get him somewhere more private. Standing in the middle of a room of reporters was not where they needed to hash this out—especially if she wanted to keep hidden the fact that he was the father of her unborn child.

"Come on," she said, making an executive decision to get them both out of there before things got even messier than they already were.

She grabbed his arm and propelled him toward the staircase situated in the left corner of the building. She'd get him outside to the back parking lot. Since the *Times'* staff had been cut down to a fraction of its former size, no one needed to park back there anymore.

He seemed to be somewhat recovered by the time they made it down the stairs and out of the building. Or at least recovered enough to ask, "It's mine?"

"Of course it's yours. Otherwise I wouldn't have felt the need to call you and leave you that voice mail."

"I swear, I didn't get the voice mail. If I had, I would have called you. I would have—" He broke off, shook his head. "So you're eighteen weeks along, then?"

"You came up with that number pretty quick," she told him, surprised that he remembered exactly when they'd met.

"I'm not the one who walked away."

"What's that supposed to mean?"

"It means, I wanted to see you again. I texted

you numerous times trying to get you to respond. You're the one who chose not to."

He was right. She knew he was right, but still, she couldn't let it go. "If you were so interested in me, why didn't you call me back when I called you? Even if you didn't get the voice mail, you had to have seen that I called."

For the first time since he'd shown up in her office like some kind of avenging angel, he wouldn't look her in the eye. Which told her everything she needed to know even before he said, "I erased your number. If you called—"

"When I called," she corrected him.

"When you called," he conceded, "you would have come up as an unknown number."

Well, if that didn't tell her exactly where she stood with the man who was the father of her child, nothing else would. She'd spent weeks, months, obsessively rereading his texts while he'd simply erased her from his life.

Then again, that was about par for the course with her, wasn't it? Growing attached when she knew she shouldn't and then being shown, again and again, that she didn't matter at all.

"Right. Of course." She tried to sound flippant, but from the look on his face she wasn't carrying it off nearly as well as she'd hoped to. "That's fine. Perfect, really, just go back to that."

"Go back to what?"

"You living your life, me living mine and never the twain shall meet."

He looked at her as if she'd lost her mind. "I hate to break it to you, Desi, but the twain has already met. And it made a baby when it did."

"You say that like I'm supposed to be surprised by the consequences of our one night together. I'm the one who's been carrying this kid for the last eighteen weeks. And I'm the one who's going to have to deal with it after it's born. So you can take all your 'we made a baby' crap and go back where you came from."

"You don't really think it's going to be that easy, do you?"

"I don't see why it has to be complicated. You go about living your life exactly as you always have and I'll figure out what to do about the baby."

"As we've already established, you're eighteen

weeks along. Which means you've already decided what to do about the baby. And if you're not having an abortion—"

"I'm not! So you're out of luck on that front."

Nic made a low, angry sound deep in his throat, shoved a frustrated hand through his hair. "Are you being deliberately obtuse? I said it was obvious that you've made up your mind to have the baby and you read that as I want you to get an abortion? What's wrong with you?"

She nearly laughed. If she had a dollar for every time someone had asked her that question in her life…well, she wouldn't be working a crappy entry-level journalism job, that's for sure. "Look, I don't even know why we're having this discussion. It's not your problem—"

"Not my problem?" he squawked.

"Exactly. Not your problem. My job isn't great but it's got good benefits and my dad's life insurance left me pretty well off when he died. So you don't have to worry that I want something from you, because I don't. I know this is my baby and—"

"Your baby?"

She glared at him, totally exasperated by his continued interruptions when she was trying so hard to get through this conversation without crying. Since she'd gotten pregnant, the hormones had her emotions all over the place.

"You know, you're really beginning to sound like a parrot."

"And you're beginning to sound like a lunatic. That baby you're carrying is as much mine as it is yours and—"

"Really? As much yours as mine? Possession is nine-tenths of the law, Nic, and right now he's inside my body, so…" She gave a little shrug to underscore her meaning—and to irritate the hell out of him. Judging from the way he was suddenly grinding his teeth together, it was working.

"It's a he? You know it's a he already?"

She almost lied, almost told him she didn't know. From the time she'd found out about the baby, but particularly after she'd called Nic and not gotten a response, she'd begun to think of this baby as exclusively hers. Someone she could take care of, someone she could love. Someone who would never go to sleep wondering where she was or when he would see her again.

And now, Nic was here. Talking about the baby as if he was already invested in him or something. She didn't trust it…and she didn't trust Nic.

But lying about it just to hurt him wasn't right, either. And so she nodded, reluctantly. "Yes, it's a boy."

His eyes glazed over at the confirmation and, for long seconds, he seemed dazed. A little out of it.

"Wow. It just got real, you know? We're having a boy."

She really didn't like the sound of that. "*I'm* having a boy."

"Are we back to that? Seriously?" He looked so disappointed that it struck a chord deep inside her. Made her squirm a little uncomfortably under his scrutiny—and under the realization that here was a man who seemed to take his responsibilities seriously. A man who wouldn't just run away from his child at the first sign of trouble.

But how did she know that, really? He'd just found out she was pregnant, so of course he was interested. Of course he wanted to be involved. But that didn't mean he'd thought it through, didn't mean he wasn't going to balk once the truth settled in.

Just the thought had her backing up and cupping a protective hand over the soft swell of her baby. "Back to it? I don't think we ever left it," she told him. "This is *my* son."

"*Our* son."

"*My* son. He—"

"God." Nic ran a frustrated hand through his hair in a motion that was becoming familiar to her, even in the short time they'd spent together. "Why are you being so obstinate about this?" he exploded. "I don't get you. I really don't. First you don't answer me when I try to get in touch with you after our night together. Then you write that assassination article and try to ruin my family's company based on a bunch of lies. And now? Now you're trying to cut me out of our kid's life before he's even born. I don't get it. What did I ever do to you to make you hate me this much?"

"I don't hate you," she told him as guilt spread through her. She tried to cut it out, to nip it in the bud, but it wasn't so easy to do when he was looking at her as if she'd just ruined Santa Claus, the Easter Bunny and the Tooth Fairy all at the same time.

"Really? Because it sure seems like you do from where I'm sitting." He shook his head, then turned his back on her and started to walk away.

Her heart dropped. He was leaving already, giving up. Which was fine, she told herself. Better now than after the baby was born. Or after she'd come to depend on him.

But it turned out, he wasn't going far. Just to the fence a few yards away. She watched as he stood there for long seconds, head bowed and hands shoved in his pockets. The guilt burning inside her got a little harder to ignore.

"Look," she said, taking a few tentative steps

in his direction. "Me writing that article has nothing to do with you."

He looked at her as if she was crazy. "You wrote an exposé about my family. You all but crucified my brother with the vicious lies of a source you won't stop protecting. It doesn't get any more 'about me' than that."

"They weren't lies."

He snorted. "Yeah. Keep telling yourself that. For a journalist, you sure don't seem to give a shit about truth."

Anger flashed through her, replacing the guilt. "You don't know anything about me!"

"Because you won't talk to me. Jesus, you're halfway done with your pregnancy and you didn't even tell me about it."

"I told you—"

"In a voice mail? In one lousy voice mail? Who does that?" He turned on her then, stalking toward her like the predator she was sure he was.

"I was pregnant with a stranger's baby! What else was I supposed to do?"

"You were supposed to answer my texts!" he roared. "You were supposed to talk to me about that bastard's accusations against Bijoux. You were supposed to get in my face about this pregnancy and make me hear you."

"That's not how I do things." She didn't beg for attention, not now, not anymore. And certainly not from a man who meant nothing to her.

"How? Reasonably? Honestly? Like an adult? Yeah, believe me, I'm getting that's not your way."

"Screw you!" Her own anger roared back to life. "You exploit children and consumers. You get rich off blood diamonds. You lie every day of your life. Who the hell are you to judge me?" She'd been so disappointed when the allegations had proved to be true, had been so hurt even though she'd known it was a ridiculous response. But he'd seemed like such a good guy that night at his house. Had seemed so perfect. To find out that he actually dealt with monsters just to turn a profit, just to go from a billionaire to a bigger billionaire…it had wounded her way more than it should have.

"You don't listen to anybody, do you?" he demanded incredulously. "You believe what you want and do your own thing and to hell with the consequences. To hell with the truth. How do you plan on being a news reporter with an attitude like that?"

His words were a slap across the face, a hit at the deepest, most sensitive part of her soul. "I *am* a news reporter."

"You're a child playing at being a grown-up." He shook his head, shoved his hands deep in his pockets as he took a steadying breath. "You know what? We're not getting anywhere with this. Why don't you go upstairs, read the file I gave you and talk to your managing editor, who's got a copy of it by now. Then figure out what you want to do and call me. We'll talk then."

"Yeah, right, I'll be sure to do that. Maybe I'll even leave a voice mail."

His face darkened and for a second it looked as if he was going to tell her off, once and for all. But in the end, he swallowed whatever obnoxious thing he'd thought of saying and simply told her, "Call me when you want to talk."

"I'm never going to want to talk to you."

"Well, that's too bad, isn't it? Because that's *my* baby you're carrying and I *will* be a part of his life. In fact, the only question from where I'm standing is, will you?"

The words were his parting shot and then he turned, walking away from her. Leaving her staring after him with her mouth open and fear clawing at her throat. She'd been around the block enough times to recognize a threat when she heard one.

For a second, she couldn't quite figure out how she'd gotten to this point. That morning, she'd woken up a soon-to-be single mother and she'd been okay with that. No, she'd been more than okay. She'd been happy with it. Fast-forward six hours, and the man who had fathered her child, a man she didn't even know, had just threatened to take that baby from her. And he was rich enough to do it.

"Hey!" she called, but he didn't turn around. Didn't so much as flinch to acknowledge that he heard her. "Nic!" She started after him, but before she could take more than two steps, her phone buzzed with a text. She glanced down at it, then froze when she saw Malcolm's words. "Bijoux article canceled. Source a hoax. See me ASAP."

Nine

Nic climbed into his car and roared out of the parking lot with no intention of stopping until he was several miles away from Desi Maddox and the *Los Angeles Times*. Running might be a juvenile reaction, but if he'd stood there arguing with her for much longer he would have said something he regretted. And since she was the mother of his child—*his child*—that didn't seem like the best course of action. For any of their sakes.

For once, LA traffic cooperated with him and as he sped through the streets he tried to calm down, tried to wrap his head around the fact that not only had he found Desi after all these months, but that he was also about to become a father. A *father*. The word reverberated in his head, the weight of it pressing in on him from all sides.

In a little less than five months, he would be a father. To a bouncing baby boy. And then what? He didn't know the first thing about parenting. How could he, when his own father had set such a shiningly bad example?

Then again, maybe Nic knew more than he thought. If he just did the opposite of everything his own father had done, he could probably win a father-of-the-year award.

He kept driving, sliding his Porsche in and out of traffic as he tried not to panic. It wasn't that he didn't want to parent his son, wasn't that he was afraid of the responsibility of it. Because he wasn't—no matter what Desi had concocted in her head about him being a soulless monster with a Peter Pan complex. That wasn't the case. He was more than willing to step up to the plate here, more than willing to take care of his child.

He was just terrified of screwing it up. Of

making mistakes that hurt his kid the way his father had hurt him and Marc. He didn't want to do that. Didn't want to be the guy who let his family down over and over and over again.

Lost in thought, he cruised through a yellow light as it turned red. Horns blared at him from both sides of the cross-traffic, and he waved a hand in silent apology even as he decided he should probably pull over before he caused an accident.

Griffith Park and Observatory was only a couple of blocks ahead of him, so he angled his way through traffic, moving to the right lane so he could make the turn into the parking lot. But once there, he couldn't just sit. His thoughts were too momentous, too overwhelming. He needed to be doing something or he would be crushed under the weight of them.

He climbed out of the car and headed for the park. If nothing else, he could walk. Nothing like a shot of nature in the middle of a crowded city to help a guy clear his head.

But as he walked, things only got more muddled. Oh, not the fact that he was going to be a father to this baby. That part he was crystal clear about. His kid, his responsibility.

But the rest of it…yeah, the rest of it was a hell of a lot murkier.

What kind of father would he be?

How would he avoid hurting his own child the way his dad had hurt him?

How would he get past the wall Desi had built around herself and get her to talk to him—and listen to him?

How were the two of them going to build some kind of secure family unit for their child when she seemed to hate him? When she believed the worst of him? When she wanted nothing to do with him?

He'd lived that life, caught between two parents who hated each other and used their children as weapons. There was no way he would let that happen to his kid. No way he would let his son grow up the same way he and Marc had.

But how was Nic going to stop it? How was he going to convince Desi that she could trust him not to hurt her or the baby? And speaking of trust, how the hell was *he* ever going to trust *her* again after everything she'd done?

He was willing to accept that she'd believed the wrong source, that she'd bought whatever ridiculous bill of goods had been sold to her. But she was an investigative journalist—albeit a green one judging from the lack of bylines he'd found when researching her. It was her job to dig for facts. Her job to talk to people on both sides of the issue as she tried to figure out who was telling the truth.

She hadn't done that. Despite the fact that they'd spent what he'd thought was a fairly spectacular night together, despite the fact that she was carrying the baby who in time would be heir to Bijoux, she'd had no problem writing an article that would have brought his family's company to its knees. And she hadn't even had the decency to give him a heads-up, let alone contact him to get his side of the story.

How much did she have to hate him to do something like that? And why? What had he done to her except give her seven orgasms—not that he'd been counting—and try to see her again? He'd liked her, really liked her…at least until she'd done all this.

As he walked, he went over the night they'd spent together, searching for something he could have done to set her off. She'd freaked out a little when he'd gotten her phone number, but they'd compromised. He'd played by the rules she set. And still she'd nearly destroyed him.

It didn't make sense.

"Daddy! Daddy! Push me higher!"

The high-pitched squeal got his attention, followed by the sound of deep male laughter. He glanced over toward the playscape, saw a man about his own age pushing a small boy on the swings. The kid was adorable, dark, wild curls and big brown eyes and the biggest smile Nic had ever seen.

"Faster, Daddy, faster!"

The man laughed again, then did as his son requested.

Nic didn't mean to stare, but he couldn't look away. They both looked so happy, the kid and the dad, who looked as if there was nowhere in the world he'd rather be.

Nic wasn't sure how long he stood there, but it was long enough to have the dad giving him a weird look. Great. He'd gone from human rights violator to park pervert in under an hour. It was shaping up to be one hell of a day.

"Sorry," he said, putting a little more distance between him and the kid. "I just found out I'm… um, expecting…an, uh, boy." What was wrong with him that he was tripping over his own tongue? That never happened to him. He was the guy who always had a joke or a story, the one who could put anyone at ease. And yet, here he was, trying to form a simple sentence about the fact that he, too, was going to be a father, and he ended up sounding like a blathering idiot.

But blathering idiot must be the language of fathers everywhere, because, somehow the guy got what Nic was saying. The suspicious look disappeared from his face, giving way to a grin that was a tad sympathetic. "You just found out you and your wife are expecting a boy?" he said.

Not quite, but it was close enough that Nic was willing to go with it. "Yeah. It's…"

"Intense," the other guy filled in.

"Yes. Exactly. Totally intense. I can't quite wrap my head around it yet."

"Daddy, higher!" the kid said again.

"Any higher and your mother will have my head," the guy responded. But Nic noticed that he pushed the boy a little bit harder, let him go a little bit higher. "Yeah, it's crazy. But it's great, too, you know. Because—" he nodded toward his son "—you get this awesome kid out of the deal."

"I can see. How old is he?"

"Just turned four."

"He's great."

The guy's chest puffed out a little. "He is, isn't he? A bit of a daredevil, always wanting to go faster or climb higher. He keeps us on our toes."

"I bet."

"Slower, Daddy!"

"Slower?" The man looked down at his son in surprise.

"I want to go on the slide now."

"Oh, sure." Nic watched as the man carefully stopped the swing and helped his son off. "You want to go on that slide over there?" he asked, pointing to the largest one on the playscape.

"No. I want to do the big one. Over there." The kid pointed to a huge, curved slide obviously meant for older kids.

"Of course you do." The dad rolled his eyes, but he held out a hand for the kid and the boy took it. "Let's go." He glanced back at Nic as they started to walk away. "Hey, good luck with the baby."

"Thanks. I appreciate that."

"You'll need it. It's the craziest thing you'll ever do. But also the best."

And then he scooped his kid up onto his shoulders and took off running across the park while the little boy shrieked in delight.

Nic stood where he was for long seconds, staring after them until they reached the other playscape. Then as the kid climbed up the slide and his dad climbed up right behind him, Nic felt himself calm down. Everything was going to be fine. He might not know anything about parenting yet, but he had five months to learn the basics. And a lifetime to learn the rest of it.

Desi had better get on board. He was willing to take a backseat, willing to do things her way. As long as her way didn't involve cutting him out completely. Because she was carrying his kid—his son—and while he was willing to compromise, the one thing he wasn't willing to do was walk away. The sooner she accepted that, the better off they would all be.

How had she screwed up this badly? Desi stared at the evidence on the desk in front of her, sorted through it for what had to be the fiftieth time as she wrapped her mind around the fact that she had made a terrible mistake.

Nic had brought all kinds of documentation with him, including page after page of chemical analysis of the diamonds sold by Bijoux. Diamonds whose environmental coating and chemical thumbprint matched exactly those being dug up in Canadian diamond mines. Not African mines. Canadian. All of which were conflict-free and responsibly sourced.

That wasn't all the evidence Nic had brought, though it was certainly damning enough con-

sidering it was signed by one of the top con-
flict-diamond experts in the world. But he'd also
brought affidavits from the foremen at each of
the mines, explaining the amount of diamonds
each mine yielded and how many pounds of diamonds had gone to Bijoux in the preceding three
years. Amounts that matched Bijoux's certified
goods received records.

He had done all his homework, had provided
the paper with everything he could possibly
need to debunk her story. And maybe she still
wouldn't believe it no matter what he said—documents could be forged after all—except Malcolm had spent the past few days running her
source to ground. After Darlene had spoken with
Nic last week about the article and he had been
so adamant about filing a libel claim if they published the information, Malcolm had wanted to
triple-check her source.

Which she'd done herself after he'd given his
information to Desi. But she must have missed
something because early this morning Malcolm
had talked with him. And had somehow managed to get from the man what she couldn't. An

admission that he had forged the documents he'd given her—from Bijoux and from the two diamond mines in Africa—in order to make it look as if Marc and Nic Durand were dirty.

All of it, forged. All of it, lies. Pages and pages of forgeries that she had bought hook, line and sinker. Because she'd wanted the story to be real—had needed the story to be real so she could write the article and move her career away from dresses and into real news. And to hell with whether or not she wrecked the lives of two innocent men. To hell if she brought down an entire business—and an entire newspaper—with her mistakes. She'd needed to get the scoop.

How could she have been so stupid? So gullible? So anxious to get the information that she'd overlooked her source's tells. And now that she looked back on it, there had been many. She'd just been so caught up in getting the story and not disappointing Malcolm, in getting the truth—ha, wasn't that a joke—that she'd looked past them. She'd made excuses for them in her own mind.

The source was nervous.

The source was a little confused but once he calmed down, he sorted it out.

The source was doing a brave thing coming forward and blowing the whistle, but he was just an amateur. Of course he hadn't known exactly what she'd need for the story.

God, she was such a fool. And the worst kind of fool—the arrogant kind who refused to see, let alone admit, when she was wrong. Just thinking about what she'd said to Nic when he'd tried to hand her the documents… She'd had in her hands the proof that he was none of those things but she'd been too stubborn to look at it. Too stubborn to admit that maybe, just maybe, she'd been wrong.

And now, the story she'd worked so hard on was dead. Malcolm told her it wasn't her fault, told her Candace—the more experienced reporter he'd put on the case to work with her—had missed the same things she had. Which was true. Candace had.

But Candace hadn't spent the time on this story that Desi had.

Candace didn't know it the way she did.

Candace hadn't been trained at an early age by Alan Maddox, one of the best investigative journalists who had ever lived.

If Candace had made a mistake, it was in trusting Desi, who had assured her over and over again that the information they had was legit.

Which it wasn't. Not at all. Not even a little bit.

So now, here she was, back in the society pages—for a little while anyway. Malcolm assured her that her job wasn't in jeopardy, but with a screwup of this magnitude, how could it not be? If that story had run—if Malcolm and Darlene had been just a little less conscientious—the paper would be in really hot water right now. And Bijoux would be under siege from everyone from the press to human rights organizations to consumer groups to lawyers bringing civil suits on behalf of clients who'd purchased Bijoux diamonds…the horrors would have gone on and on.

And it would have been all her fault.

Yet Nic had still wanted to talk to her, had still wanted to listen to her. And in her utter and complete arrogance, she'd driven him away. Worse, she'd backed him into a corner where he thought that the only choice he had was to fight her—for his company and for their baby.

Nice job, Desi. Somehow she'd managed to mess her life up so royally, so completely, that she could not even begin to imagine how to fix it. She didn't even know if fixing it was possible.

But she also knew she had to try. She'd made this mess, and while Malcolm was helping her clean it up on the professional level, she owed it to Nic, and their baby, to try to fix it on the personal front, as well.

Which meant she would have to call him. And explain the situation. And grovel—a lot. God. She closed her eyes, lowered her head to the desk. She hated groveling. She really, really, really hated groveling—especially when she was the one in the wrong.

But she was smart enough—and woman enough—to admit that she had brought it on herself. She was the one who hadn't listened to Nic and she was the one who was so wrapped up in her investigation, and the kind of man she'd thought he was, that she'd left one voice mail for him and then given up. Even though she was carrying his baby. And even though she'd known—though she would deny it to her dying day—that there was a good chance that after she'd ignored him for weeks that he wouldn't listen to any message she left.

Just because she knew what she needed to do didn't mean it was easy. Desi gave herself five minutes to sulk and then did what she had to do. She put on her big-girl panties and called Nic.

Ten

He brought her to one of his favorite restaurants in LA, a little trattoria in the heart of Beverly Hills. He liked it because the food was great and the owner's brother had worked for Bijoux for years, but he could tell the moment they walked into the place that he had definitely chosen wrong.

Though Desi didn't say anything, it was obvious that she was uncomfortable. He thought about ignoring her discomfort so as not to make it any worse, but they already had a lot of strikes against them. This dinner was supposed to be about finding some common ground, and if it would make her feel better to go someplace else, then he was more than willing to do that for her.

But when he asked if she'd feel more comfortable at one of the other restaurants on the street, she just shrugged and said, "This is fine."

"Are you sure? Because if you don't like Italian—"

"Everyone likes Italian food," she told him with a slightly exasperated roll of her eyes. "That's not the problem."

"Then what is?"

"This place is expensive."

"Don't worry about that. I asked you out—"

"I don't want your money. That's not why I called you tonight. And it's definitely not why I'm keeping the baby. I just want to say that up front and you need to believe me. I don't need or want you to take me to fancy restaurants and spend a lot on me."

"Believe me," he answered with a smirk, "I am well aware that you don't want my money, Desi. Otherwise you wouldn't have written an article guaranteed to cost me billions."

She flushed, and for the first time since they

sat down, she refused to look him in the eye. "I know I already said it, but I'm really sorry about that. I wasn't out to get you. I just believed the wrong person and…" Her voice trailed off as she ducked her head.

He didn't like this new, humble version of her. Yes, ten hours ago he'd pretty much been out for D. E. Maddox's blood. But that was before he realized D. E. Maddox was also Desi. The woman he'd spent the most sensual, sexy, satisfying night of his life with. The woman who met him point for point with strength and attitude. The woman who, he now knew, was carrying his child.

"Look, why don't we just start over?" he told her, reaching across the table and resting his hand on top of hers.

"Start over?" She looked incredulous. "I'm nearly five months pregnant with your son. I think it's a little late to try starting over."

He laughed. "I don't mean that I want to walk up to you in a bar and introduce myself to you while we pretend we don't know each other. I just mean, let's have a clean slate. Leave whatever's in the past in the past and deal with where we are now without any of the junk from before messing it up."

"You want us to just forget everything?"

"Why not?"

"Do you think we can do that?"

"Do you not?"

She laughed then. "Are we seriously back to this? Answering each other's questions with more questions?"

"Hey. I asked the first question—you've just been piling question on question after that."

"I'm pretty sure that's not how it happened." She eyed him skeptically. "But I'm willing to take the blame this time, as a peace offering."

He felt himself relax, really relax, for the first time in days. Desi was here with him, they were having a conversation that didn't involve sniping at each other—and that he hoped would, soon enough, also include real communication. Plus, his company was safe. At this exact moment in time, what else could he ask for?

After giving their order to the waiter—chicken picatta for him and angel-hair pasta for her—

the two of them made small talk. About LA, about the weather, about a band they had both recently seen in concert. But as the meal went on, Nic grew increasingly frustrated. Not because he minded talking to Desi about that stuff— she was smart and funny and interesting, and if things were normal he'd be happy to spend the evening laughing and flirting with her over their dimly lit table.

But things weren't normal, and while he tended to be pretty easygoing about most things that didn't involve Bijoux, he wasn't okay with being easygoing about this. Not when she was carrying his child. And not when they had so much to figure out.

By the time their meal had been cleared and he had ordered dessert—she had passed, but he hoped to tempt her with some lemon marscapone cheesecake—he was more than ready to talk about their son and what arrangements they were going to make for him.

Desi seemed to sense his mood, because she stopped right in the middle of the story she was telling and looked at him.

He didn't like the apprehension in her eyes, or the way her body tensed as if she was waiting for a blow. He'd spent his whole life charming women. The last thing he wanted was for the mother of his child—for Desi—to be afraid of him.

Reaching across the table, he slid his hand down her hair. She startled at his touch, but he didn't move his hand away. Instead he pushed an errant lock behind her ear. Then he skimmed a finger down the soft curve of her cheek.

Her eyes drifted shut at the first touch of his skin on hers and she swayed a little. Leaned her cheek into his hand. And, just that easily, the fire that had burned so hotly on the night they met reignited.

It had been eighteen weeks since he'd held her, eighteen weeks since he'd kissed his way across her shoulders and down the delicate curve of her spine. But he still remembered what she felt like against him, around him. Still remembered the way she moaned when he slipped inside her and the way she raked her fingers down his back when she came.

"Let me take you back to your place," he said, his voice hoarse with a desire he didn't even try to hide. "Let me make you feel good."

Her eyes flew open at his words, and in their depths he saw the same arousal he was feeling, the same need. But there was a reluctance there, too, that spoke of confusion and conflict, and he knew—no matter how much he wanted her— he couldn't have her. Not now. Not when things were still so unsettled between them.

So he pulled back, let his hand fall away from her cheek.

"I'm sorry," she said. "I've made such a mess of things."

She had, but he wasn't going to blame her for it. Not when he'd made his share of mistakes, too. He was the one who had erased her number from his phone. He was the one who hadn't been diligent about listening to his messages and had ended up missing the most important voice mail of his life.

"That's why we're starting over. No more messes to clean up, from either of us." Because his head was still a little cloudy with desire—

and it wasn't the only part of his anatomy to feel that way—he leaned back in his chair and took a long sip of water while he tried to get his thoughts together.

"Look, I know you want to talk about the baby, but I'm not sure what to say about that yet. I've spent the last three months thinking I'm going to be doing this alone and now you're here and you want to be involved. That's great, but I need time to adjust."

"I get that. I do. And we've got time to figure everything out. But I want you to know that you aren't in this alone anymore."

"I know."

"No, I don't think you do," he told her. "I don't just want to be a part of the baby's life after he's born. I want to start now. You're pregnant and, I don't know, pregnant women need things, right? If you do, I want to be there to help you out."

For long seconds, Desi didn't say anything. Which was fine, because she didn't reject his words outright. But the longer she kept him waiting, the more anxious he got. He'd already threatened her once today about the baby. He didn't want her to think he was doing it again.

But just as he opened his mouth to explain, she said, "I'm okay with that."

"You are?"

"You don't have to sound so surprised," she said with a laugh.

"I'm not. It's just… I was a real ass about the baby earlier and I'm sorry. I don't want you to think this is a part of what happened before because it's not."

"Hey, you're the one who keeps talking about a clean slate. I think that's supposed to work both ways, isn't it?"

"Yeah. I guess it is."

She nodded, then took a deep breath. Let it out slowly. "So, you want to be a part of the pregnancy?"

"Absolutely." He thought back to when he was in the park earlier, to the father and the son who'd been at the swings when he was walking by. He wanted that, more than he'd ever imagined possible, and he was going to do whatever he had to do to get it.

"Okay. I have a doctor's appointment next week. You could come to that if you want."

"I do want to. But I want more than that, as well."

"More?" She looked confused. "That's pretty much all there is at this point. A doctor's appointment once a month and then, when I'm closer to my due date, one every two weeks. And, I should probably warn you, they aren't very exciting appointments, you know? I pee on a stick, I listen to the baby's heartbeat—which, I admit, is the best part. Sometimes the doctor takes my blood. But that's it."

"It sounds pretty good to me."

"That's because you aren't the one getting stuck with needles," she told him.

"Well, thank God," he said, adding an exaggerated eye roll for effect. "I'm a crier."

"You know, I can see that about you," she said with a laugh. "You've got that look about you."

He lifted a brow at her. "I look like a crybaby?"

"You look…sensitive."

That startled a laugh out of him. "Well, I've

got to say, that's the first time anyone's ever told me *that*."

"That's because you keep your sensitive side hidden behind all that charm."

She said it as a joke, but again, there was something about the look in her eye that told him she saw more than he wanted her to. More than he wanted *anyone* to. His whole life he'd been the joker, the charmer, the easygoing one who countered Marc's intensity. He'd been the one who defused their father's temper when things started to go bad and the one who stepped between him and Marc when things *did* go bad. And he did it all with a smile.

He'd spent years honing the persona, years perfecting it until everyone who knew him believed he was *that* guy. Hell, most of the time he believed it himself. The idea that Desi saw through the mask, that she saw what no one else had ever bothered to look for, rocked him to his core.

Which was the only excuse he had for what happened next.

From that moment in the park, when he'd decided definitively what he wanted, he'd been working toward this moment. Everything he'd done since then had been geared toward making Desi trust him, geared toward making her want to go along with his suggestion. He'd even had a plan about how to broach the idea.

But as he sat here, reeling from what should have been a simple throwaway observation but somehow wasn't, he wanted nothing so much as to change the subject. To get the focus off him. So he blurted out the first thing that came to mind, not caring—until it was too late—that doing so blew his whole plan sky high.

"I want you to move in with me," he told her straight out, not even bothering to cushion the blow.

"Move in with you?" She looked at him as if he was crazy. "You can't be serious."

"I'm totally serious."

"You aren't."

He waited until the waiter stopped by to freshen their waters and drop off dessert before he said, "I am." Then he reached over and forked up a bite of cheesecake and held it out to her.

She didn't take it right away. Instead, she studied him and studied the bite of cheesecake while the second hand wound its way around his watch.

"Maybe you are," she finally said, leaning forward to take the bite off his fork. "But you shouldn't be. We don't even know each other."

She'd gotten a tiny dab of whipped cream on his very favorite part of her upper lip and he wanted nothing more than to lean forward and lick it off. The only thing holding him back was the fact that he knew it wouldn't score him any points right now—and it sure as hell wouldn't help him convince her that he wasn't angling for a roommate-with-benefits relationship…

"But it makes perfect sense. What if something happens and you need me—"

"I didn't realize you were a doctor."

"That's not what I meant."

"No, but if I need you, I can call you." She held up her phone. "That's what these really nifty smartphones are for. That is, of course, provided you actually pick up this time."

She said it as if it was a joke, but there was

an underlying bite to it that he'd have to be an idiot to miss. "Exactly my point. If we were living together, you wouldn't have to call me. I'd just be there."

She sighed heavily, then said, "Nic, look, I know this whole baby thing has thrown you for a loop today. Believe me, I get that. I've known for months and it still freaks me out. But that doesn't mean we have to do anything crazy. I understand that this is your gut reaction. But why don't you take a few days and really think about it. Make sure being involved is what you really want—"

"It is what I want. I'm not the kind of guy who runs from his responsibilities, Desi."

"But see, that shouldn't be why you decide to stick around. Only because the baby is your responsibility. You should be a part of his life because you want to be, not because you feel like you have to be."

"Now you're twisting my words. Of course I want to be a part of his life—"

"Just listen to me for a minute, okay?" It was her turn to reach across the table and put her hand on his. "You need to seriously think about this before you do anything rash. Because if you want out, it would be better if you walked away now rather than in four months or four years, when you decide you're bored."

"Why are you so sure I'm going to walk away?" he asked.

"Why are you so sure you're not?"

"And we're back to trading questions." He couldn't quite keep the frustration out of his voice.

"We are," she agreed with a small smile. "But they're important questions. And you didn't answer mine."

"Neither did you." He caught her gaze, held it, then refused to look away.

Desi blinked first, glancing up at the twinkling lights that lined the nearby windows. "I just think you need to think about things."

"I have thought about them."

"For a few *hours*!"

"Sometimes a few hours are all you need."

She rolled her eyes. "You're being completely irrational."

Her voice rose on the last couple of words, and that's when it hit him just how upset she was by this whole discussion. Oh, she was fronting, pretending she was amused and exasperated, but there was something else underneath it all. Something dark, and maybe a little afraid.

It was the fear that gave him pause, that had him sitting back in his chair, studying her as he tried to figure out what made her tick. He didn't have much luck, which was frustrating, but on this one small point, he would concede she was right. They didn't know each other, and until they did, he couldn't get a bead on her.

Which was only one more reason for them to move in together, he decided. Nothing broke down barriers like the forced intimacy of cohabitation. Instinct told him not to mention that to Desi, however, because it might send her running for the hills.

"What's it going to take," he asked, when the silence between them moved from uncomfortable to unbearable, "for you to agree to move in with me?"

"Nothing," she answered immediately. "Because it's not going to happen. Beyond all the reasons why two people who don't know each other shouldn't be moving in together, there are also the logistics. You live and work in San Diego. I live and work in LA. There's no way I'm driving three hours, in traffic, to work and home every day. It isn't going to happen."

"If that's your biggest objection, forget about it. We can totally fix it."

"How can we fix it? Even all your money isn't enough to make LA traffic move during rush hour."

"Maybe not, but there are other ways to get to work besides a car."

"Like what?"

"Like a helicopter." He drained his water glass in one long sip. "See, problem solved."

"Yes, but I don't have a helicopter."

"Maybe not, but I've got three."

"Look," she said, throwing her napkin down on the table and standing up. "We're done talking about this. I'm going to the bathroom and when I come back we need a new topic of conversation. Because if we don't, I'm out of here.

And I can promise that neither the baby nor I will be pleased about looking for a bus stop in Beverly Hills."

Eleven

By the time she got back from the bathroom—where she'd had more than a few WTF moments—Nic had paid the bill and was waiting to escort her out to the car. He hadn't, however, come up with a new topic of conversation. Instead, he had a new twist on the old one.

"So," he said as he slid behind the wheel of a car that cost significantly more than she made in a year and started the engine, "I think I've found a solution."

"I didn't know we had a problem," she answered drily.

He ignored her. "You don't want to move in with me, so why don't I move in with you?"

She burst out laughing. She knew it was rude, especially when he looked so pleased with his suggestion, but she couldn't help it. The idea of a multibillionaire slumming it in her tiny fourth-story walk-up in Los Feliz was hilarious, especially considering the fact that his *pantry* was bigger than her whole apartment.

The look he gave her as he backed out of the parking space was decidedly disgruntled. "I don't see what's so funny."

"Really? You don't?"

"No."

She thought about enlightening him, but the truth was, he might actually have hit on the perfect solution for getting him off her back about this. He wouldn't last a day in her apartment, so why not let him move in? The first morning he couldn't get hot water or the air-conditioning went on the fritz, he'd be out of there. Billionaire playboys born with silver spoons in their mouths rarely knew how to rough it. Not that she'd met

that many billionaire playboys—or even more
than one, really—but she was certain her opin-
ion would hold up.

"Okay, fine," she said as he pulled into traffic.
"You can move in with me."

"Seriously?" He glanced over at her before
fastening his eyes back on the road. "You mean
it?"

"I do. If you're willing to move into my place—
which, I'm warning you, is small—then who am
I to tell you no? But we need to lay down some
ground rules if we're going to do this."

His smile quickly turned perplexed. "Ground
rules?"

"Yeah, like who gets the bathroom when and
who does what chores and no sex. You know,
the usual."

Now he was frowning and it was all she could
do not to crack up again. It was wrong of her to
be enjoying this so much, but she couldn't help
it. After all the tension of the day, messing with
him was a welcome relief.

"Do you have a problem with any of those
rules?" she asked when she'd finally managed to

choke down her mirth. The last thing she wanted him to know was how utterly and completely she expected this to fail.

"Well, you can have the bathroom whenever you want and I'll hire someone to do the cleaning and I'll do the rest of the chores. But the no-sex rule—I'm not really okay with that one, no."

"Oh." She kept her voice as innocent as possible. "That's kind of a deal breaker for me, to be honest."

"But we've already had sex. And—" he made a point of glancing at her stomach "—you're pregnant. So, I'm not really sure what the point would be of abstaining."

"The point is what I said back at the restaurant. I don't know you. And my one and only one-night stand excluded, I'm not in the habit of sleeping with men I don't know. So, yeah, it's a deal breaker."

"I'm your only one-night stand?"

She did laugh then, at the sheer ridiculousness of his response. "Seriously, that's what you got out of what I said? That you're my one and only?"

"No, I heard all of it. But that was definitely the most interesting part."

"Of course it was," she said with a snort. "You are such a guy."

He shot her an amused look. "I never claimed to be anything else, sweetheart."

"Don't call me that." The words were instantaneous and forceful, welling up from a place she hadn't thought of in years.

"What?" He looked mystified. "Sweetheart?"

"Yes, that. Don't *ever* call me that."

"Sure." He held up a placating hand. "I'm sorry. I didn't mean to upset you."

"You didn't upset me," she contradicted him.

He didn't respond, but the silence spoke louder than any words ever could. He knew she was lying, knew she'd had a strong and immediate reaction to that word. And still he wasn't calling her on it. She didn't know if that endeared him to her or just pissed her off.

It took a few minutes for the awkwardness to wear off, but Nic finally asked for directions to her apartment.

She kept her voice light and relaxed when she

gave them, and eventually the last of the tension eased away. At least until he'd parked his car and started following her up the stairs to her apartment.

"Is there an elevator?" he asked after they'd started on the third flight.

"Nope," she answered cheerfully.

"That's going to be a problem for you the last couple months of your pregnancy, don't you think?" She could practically hear the wheels turning in his head as he tried to figure out how to use this to get her out of the apartment and into his house.

Not that she would let that happen.

"I already asked my doctor about it. She said it should be fine—exercise is good for me and the baby. She did warn that if I ended up having a C-section, I wouldn't be allowed to go up and down them the first few weeks, but at this point there's nothing to indicate I'll have anything but a normal delivery." She smiled at him blithely.

"So, there are early indicators that someone might need a C-section?"

"Yes, but I don't have any of them." She

reached for his hand, squeezed it, as they finally made it to her door. "Relax, Nic. Everything's fine with my pregnancy so far. It's totally boring, which is a good thing, my doctor assures me."

He still didn't look convinced, but he let it go as she unlocked her apartment door. "Are you coming in?" she asked after she'd stepped into her three-foot-by-three-foot entryway.

"Do you want me to?" He watched her face closely as he waited for her answer. "You look pretty tired."

She felt pretty tired. The day had brought so many emotional highs and lows she felt as if she'd run a marathon—or maybe two. The exhaustion of her first trimester had disappeared a few weeks ago, but that didn't mean she wasn't tired at the end of every day. As Stephanie had told Desi the other day when she'd been caught napping in the break room, making another person was pretty hard work.

But she and Nic still had things to talk about—such as her ground rules and whether or not he really wanted to do this now that he'd seen just how small her apartment was. "It's fine," she told him, stepping back so he could enter.

He must have read the tiredness on her face, though, because he shook his head. "I think I'll get going. Let you get some rest." He pulled his phone out of his pocket, then looked a little shamefaced as he asked, "Can I get your number again? I promise not to erase it this time."

"I guess we'll just have to wait and see about that," she said.

She'd meant it as a joke, but his eyes shot to hers. He was deadly serious—deadly earnest—when he told her, "I'm not going anywhere, Desi."

Yeah, that's what they all said. And somehow it had never quite worked out that way for her. Oh, they all had a really good reason for why they had to leave—or why she had to—but the results were always the same. Her, alone, trying to pick up the pieces of a heart broken by too many people too many ways and too many times.

But she was done with that, she told herself

as she rattled off her phone number. Done with opening herself up to someone only to watch the person walk away. So she'd give Nic a chance, she'd let him into this baby's life, but that was it. There was no way she would let herself depend on him. No way she would let him hurt her when he finally decided to walk away.

It had taken him eight weeks to erase her from his phone when she didn't answer his texts. Once the baby was born and everything got harder, how long would it take him to leave them both?

Not very long was her bet. Not very long, at all.

"Get some sleep," he told her after saving her number. "I'll call you tomorrow and we'll talk about the logistics of me moving in. I want to do it as soon as possible."

"How soon is that?" she asked warily.

"This coming weekend, if that's okay with you. I'd do it sooner, but I know you have work and the last thing I want to do is rock the boat for you at the paper."

She snorted. "Yeah, well, I think that boat has already been rocked pretty hard today." The memory made her wince even as it brought the guilt back. She'd almost ruined Nic and his brother, almost brought down their entire company, and yet here he was, telling her that he didn't want to disrupt her job. If things had been reversed, she'd probably be calling for his head on a silver platter, baby or no baby.

"I'm sorry," she told him. "An apology is not close to being enough when my carelessness nearly cost you and your family everything, but I don't know what else to say."

"Clean slate, remember?" He leaned over then and pressed a lingering kiss to her forehead. "We're starting over."

Were they? His gentle, platonic kiss somehow managed to send heat sizzling along her nerve endings. Because from where she stood, it felt as if they were picking up right where they'd left off eighteen weeks before.

It was an alarming idea, considering the close quarters they would be living in. And the no-sex rule she was serious about enforcing. Chemistry between them had never been a problem, and she knew if she let him back in her bed, getting rid of him would take a hell of a lot longer than it would otherwise. After all, how would they find out how incompatible they were in real life if they never actually got out of bed?

She knew this, understood it, even believed it wholeheartedly. And still her body swayed toward him, still she tilted her face up for a kiss that shouldn't happen. Still she longed to feel his hard, calloused hands brushing over her skin.

Nic's eyes darkened as she stared up into them. They turned the same green as the storm-tossed Atlantic, and she felt more of her resistance give way. If he kissed her right now…if he *touched* her, she wasn't sure she'd have the strength to say no.

But in the end, he did neither. Instead, he took a couple of steps back, until he was no longer in touching distance. He gave her a sweet smile— sweeter than anything she thought a guy like him was capable of—and said, "Go get some sleep. I'll call you in the morning and we'll get the details of my move worked out. We'll both feel better then."

She was glad he sounded certain, because suddenly she was anything but. Still, she nodded, gave him the best smile she could muster. "Yeah. We'll talk tomorrow."

They stood there for several long seconds more, neither of them taking the first move to break the new and tenuous connection between them. All she had to do was step back and close the door. All he had to do was turn and walk away. And still they silently watched each other. Silently imagined what might be coming next… for both of them.

Despite her best intentions, she felt herself softening toward him. Felt herself wondering if maybe he would stick around for a while—for the baby, of course, not for her.

But after everything she'd been through, after all the people she'd had to tell goodbye over the years, even thinking he might stay for the baby felt like a weakness. More, it felt like a betrayal.

And so she found the will to step back.

Found the will to whisper a soft good-night.

And somehow she even found the will to close the door in Nic's very handsome, very sexy, very sweet face.

* * *

By Sunday, Desi still wasn't over her moment of weakness. In fact, she'd spent the better part of the week berating herself for it even as she felt herself falling a little more under Nic's spell with each day that passed.

He'd called her twice a day, every day, just to check on her. He had a small basket of fresh fruit delivered to her doorstep each morning and a healthy, delicious dinner delivered each night. He even drove up from San Diego one day to meet her for lunch so he could check on her and the baby. And through it all, he had never voiced a word of dissension at the increasingly ridiculous rules she'd insisted on making up for their living arrangement.

The guy definitely had his eye on the endgame, and that wasn't going to do. Not when he was being so nice about it. And not when she felt as if she was one small step away from getting sucked into a vortex of need and want and emotional attachment.

Wasn't going to happen.

Which was why, on this fine Sunday morning

in July, she stood in the middle of her very small kitchen watching her neighbor Serena direct her burly boyfriend and brother, telling them where in Desi's apartment they should put the French provincial sofa they were currently carrying. Not that it really mattered. The thing would dominate the room wherever they put it.

How could it not? It was huge and ugly and the most atrocious shade of hot pink she had ever seen. It was also curved and hard as a rock and would be absolutely miserable for Nic to sleep on. One night on the thing and his back would never be the same.

At another time, she might feel badly about conspiring to torture Nic while he was being so determinedly supportive, but desperate times called for desperate measures. He was moving in later that afternoon, and with the way her stupid pregnancy hormones were all out of whack, she didn't trust herself not to jump him. Or much worse, fall for him.

Which was why she'd begged Serena to let her borrow her friend's most prized piece of furniture. It would cost Desi a couple of hundred bucks and an entire day spent at the spa, but at this point, that seemed a small price to pay. Nic had to go and he had to go fast.

She would make those words her mantra and use them every time she felt her resolve weakening. Which lately seemed to be every time she saw Nic or heard his voice on the phone or even thought about him—which she was doing more and more lately.

Stupid pregnancy hormones.

By the time Nic showed up at her door with two suitcases and a laptop case filled with electronics, she was a wreck. Especially since she hadn't had anything to do but sit around and wait for him to appear.

Normally she spent Sunday mornings cleaning her apartment, but a cleaning service had shown up before she'd left for work on Thursday. When she'd tried to turn them away, thinking they'd gotten the apartment number wrong, they'd assured her that Nic had sent them. And that they'd be back every week to make sure her apartment was "spick-and-span." Their words, not hers.

When she'd tried to talk to Nic about it, to tell him she didn't need or want him to pay for a cleaning service, he'd told her it wasn't for her, it was for him. He was a total pig, he claimed, and he needed someone to clean up after him.

The fact that she could hear the laughter in his voice as he said it—and called him on it—didn't make him change his story. That was when she'd figured out what she'd only suspected when she'd gone home with him all those weeks ago—that she really had met her match.

"I cleared out half the closet for you," she told him as he made his way into the apartment. "I figured you could use that chest for stuff you didn't want to hang up." She pointed at the arts and crafts–style highboy she had found at a garage sale right out of college. She'd brought it home, stripped it and painted it a bright sunshiny yellow that she loved—and that, it turned out, clashed horribly with the hot pink French provincial sofa that now dominated her living area.

Normally she used the chest to hold her books, but for now they were in boxes under her bed. If she played her cards right, the books would be back where they belonged by Wednesday. Maybe sooner, if that couch was as uncomfortable to stretch out on as she imagined it would be.

"Thanks," he said with a smile that was way too sexy for her peace of mind. "I really appreciate that."

Guilt slithered through her, made her palms sweat and her stomach swirl. But she shoved it back down, hard. Nic had to go and he had to go now. She repeated her mantra like the lifeline it was.

"Do you need help unpacking?" she asked, reaching for one of his suitcases.

"I've got it." He held the bag away from her. "Why don't you sit down and rest while I empty these suitcases, and then I'll take you to lunch."

"I'm pregnant, Nic, not an invalid."

"True, but I am neither pregnant nor an invalid, so I beat you." He pointed to the monstrosity of a sofa without so much as batting an eye. "Now, sit."

She did her best not to cringe. Why, oh why, had she not considered the fact that he would expect her to sit on that couch? Which wasn't as bad as lying on it, obviously, but was still not good.

"I actually prefer the bar stools," she said, gesturing to the three chairs that lined the overhanging counter on the outside edge of her kitchen.

As she turned away, she thought she heard him murmur, "I bet," under his breath, but when she whirled back to look at him, his smile was perfectly innocent.

Yeah, as if she was buying that.

After grabbing her laptop off her desk, she settled at the bar to put the finishing touches on an article about the charity ball benefiting the LA Zoo that she'd attended the night before. It was due by five, but getting it in early could only help her career. Though Malcolm didn't treat her any differently, she couldn't help feeling as if she was persona non grata in the newsroom.

Or maybe that was her own sense of guilt and responsibility. Stephanie—who'd been at the *Times* for nearly ten years—had assured her that all reporters screwed up sometimes. Maybe that was true. But how many of them screwed up on

their first major assignment? When she'd asked
Stephanie that, her friend had suddenly needed
to make a phone call. Which told Desi everything she already knew.

She'd written the zoo story earlier because
she'd thought it'd be hard to work with Nic in
her apartment. After all, the place was only
about seven hundred square feet, and he was
big enough that it felt as if he took up most of it.

Yet, as he unpacked, he was as unobtrusive as
a gorgeous, six-foot-four man could be. He didn't
interrupt her, didn't ask her where he should put
his belongings. He just did his thing and let her
do hers. If she'd had a little more self-control and
actually been able to stop herself from stealing
glances at him every five seconds, she probably
would have finished proofing her article a heck
of a lot faster.

As it was, they finished their tasks at the same
time, after which Nic insisted on taking her out
to lunch to celebrate their new living arrangement. He plied her with *queso* and guacamole
and deep-fried ice cream—which was nowhere
near as disgusting as it sounded—then took her

for a walk around Griffith Park. It was crowded because it was a weekend, but it was fun all the same.

She'd spent so much of her life alone—by circumstance when she was young and by choice after she reached adulthood—that it hadn't occurred to her how nice it could be to do things with someone else. How something as simple as a walk in the park became so much more fun when there was someone to share it with.

And when they finally made it back to her apartment and she saw what she'd missed earlier—three books on pregnancy and parenting that Nic had, if judging by the bookmark placement, been spending some serious time reading—it hit her that she might be in serious trouble.

Because for the first time since she'd decided to let Nic move in, she wasn't thinking about how to get rid of him. Instead, she was thinking of ways to make him stay.

Twelve

Nic had just finished shaving early Monday morning when Desi called to him from the kitchen. "Nic! Come here! Hurry up!"

The urgency in her tone struck fear into his heart, and he rushed out of the bathroom and through the bedroom without even stopping to grab a shirt. "Are you okay?" he called as he ran through her matchbox-sized apartment. "What's wrong?"

He got to the kitchen before she could answer, and he glanced around wildly, looking for some kind of threat. But there was nothing, only Desi leaning against the kitchen counter, her hand on her stomach and a huge smile on her face.

"Is something wrong with the baby?" he asked as he crossed the kitchen and stopped directly in front of her.

"He's kicking!"

It was so not what he'd expected her to say that it took her words a few seconds to register. When they did, his gaze flew to her stomach. He'd felt that one small kick at her desk, but he'd been too surprised to appreciate it—or the fact that it happened on a regular basis. "He's kicking?"

"Yes." Rolling her eyes at his slowness, she pushed her clothes out of the way with one hand and grabbed his hand with the other. Then she brought his palm to her bare stomach and held it there.

For long moments, he didn't feel anything and he looked at Desi questioningly. But she just nodded her encouragement, her hand tightening on his. So he waited, heart pounding and breath held, to feel…something.

And then, there it was. A gentle bump against his palm.

"He kicked me!" he crowed with delight.

"Actually, I think he kicked me," she told him drily. "You're just collateral damage."

"Don't listen to your mother," he told the baby as he dropped to the ground at Desi's feet and leaned his mouth close to her gently rounded tummy. "She's just grumpy cuz she's not allowed coffee in the mornings anymore."

"Hey! Don't be calling me grumpy to the baby." Desi poked at his shoulder. "Or I won't tell you the next time he kicks."

"See, I told you she was grumpy. Mean, too." He smoothed his palm over her stomach, checking out the changes to her body since the last time he'd been this close to her. There weren't many yet, despite the fact that she was nearly halfway through her pregnancy. Just the added roundness to her tummy and the swelling of her breasts, both of which he found sexy as hell.

"You'd be mean, too, if you had to give up caffeine cold turkey."

"No doubt," he soothed, just as the baby kicked a second time.

"See! He got my hand again! I told you he was kicking me."

She snorted. "No offense, but *your* hand pretty much covers *my* entire stomach at this point."

He wasn't sure what it was that did it, but suddenly he was much less aware of the baby and much more aware of the fact that he was on his knees in front of Desi, his hand resting on the bare, silky skin of her stomach and his mouth inches away from her sex.

Once the realization set in, he couldn't stop himself from leaning forward slightly and breathing her in.

Desi stiffened against him and he froze, ready to apologize. But she didn't push him away. Instead, her hands came to rest on his shoulders, then slid slowly up his neck so that her fingers could tangle in his hair.

Desire shot through him at the first touch of her hands, and he leaned forward even more, until he closed the last scant inch between her stomach and his lips.

She groaned at his mouth on her skin, but again she didn't push him away. Instead she pulled him closer, her body arching against his as her fingers tightened in his hair. He'd read in one of the pregnancy manuals he'd picked up that women's hormones went crazy during pregnancy, which often caused a spike in their libido. If that was what was happening now, he didn't want to take advantage of it, even though his whole body ached with the need to touch her, to kiss her, to slide inside her welcoming heat and feel her clench around him.

But at the same time, he didn't want to leave her like this, either. He could feel her arousal in the way she was moving restlessly against him, could hear it in the soft sounds of distress she was making in the back of her throat. Could smell it in the sexy warmth of her skin.

"Let me make you feel good," he whispered against her skin as he skimmed his lips across her belly. "Just that. Nothing else."

"Yes," she said, her head falling back against the cabinet with a light thump. "Please, Nic. I need—"

He clamped a gentle hand over her mouth, not because he didn't want to hear the words of need pouring out, but because they were building his own arousal, making him hotter and harder than he'd been since the last time he'd had Desi's body pressed against his own. And no matter how much he wanted to make love to her right now, her words from the other night—her rules—were fresh in his head.

He didn't mind bending the rules to make her feel good, but until she told him otherwise, sex was off the table. Which would have sucked completely if he didn't at least get the benefit of watching Desi climax. She was so beautiful, so hot, so gorgeous when she came, and he'd missed seeing it more than he should have if all she'd been to him was a one-night stand.

But there was time enough to deal with that later, to try to figure out where they were going from here and how everything would end up. Right now…right now all he wanted was to get his mouth on Desi and to hear her call his name as she came.

With that thought in mind, he pressed soft kisses in a straight line up from her abdomen. When her tank top got in his way, he pulled it off with a growl and flung it over his shoulder. And there she was, soft, sun-kissed skin and full, heavy breasts. Dark pink nipples peeking between strands of long blond hair.

"Beautiful," he murmured as he looked up at her. "You're so damn beautiful, Desi."

She was looking back down at him, worrying her lower lip between her teeth. She blushed at his words, turned away, but he caught her chin in his hand and gently brought her gaze back down to his.

"Don't hide from me," he told her, underscoring his words with a soft bite to the underside of her breast.

She moaned, her eyes going blurry, and he almost lost it. Almost turned her around, bent her over the counter and took her as he'd dreamed of too many times in the past five months.

But that wasn't what she needed right now—wasn't what either of them needed—and so he tamped down the wildness inside himself and concentrated on her instead. Just her.

The changes in her body were more evident now that she was naked, her stomach round, her breasts full and swollen, her nipples bright pink and hard as rubies. She was still tan, golden, but for the first time he could see blue veins running beneath the delicate skin of her breasts.

They made her seem so fragile, so delicate, and he forced himself to be gentle as he cupped her breasts in his hands. She gasped, and he asked, "Are they sore?" before leaning in to trace the upper curves with his tongue. "The books say—"

"They're okay. A little sensitive, but if you're gentle—"

Her breath broke as he licked his way closer and closer to her nipple. Tiny, tender strokes of his tongue meant to both soothe and inflame. He took his time, was as slow and gentle as he knew how to be as he relearned her body after all the long months without her. He kissed and licked and lapped at her, learning every inch— every centimeter—of her breasts all over again.

It took only a couple of minutes before Desi was thrashing against him, her beautiful body trembling with need as she clutched at his back, his shoulders, his hair. He loved the way her hands felt on him, loved even more the way she responded to him. The way she held nothing back. The way she gave him everything.

He wanted to do that for her. Wanted to give *her* everything. Wanted to make her feel so good that even when this was over, even when she was away from him, she wouldn't remember all her reasons for why they shouldn't be together.

He wanted her to want him—to need him—the same way he needed her.

"Nic, please." She trembled against him, then bucked and arched as she tried to coax him into giving her what she wanted.

He laughed and pulled his mouth completely away, but stayed close enough that she could still feel his breath on her nipple. She moaned in response, grabbing his head in her hands and tangling her fingers in his hair as she tried to pull him back to her breast.

"Don't tease me," she pleaded.

"Baby, I haven't begun to tease you." He curled his tongue around her areola and sucked it into his mouth hard enough to have her gasping.

"Too much?" he asked, immediately softening the pressure. The last thing he wanted to do was hurt her.

"No! Please. I'm so close. I'm—" She broke off as he stripped her pajama pants down her legs and tossed them aside. "Take me," she said. "Please, Nic, I want to feel you."

"I'm right here," he told her, kissing his way down to her firm, round stomach. The noises she was making, the things she was saying—they were revving him up, making it harder for him to be careful. Harder for him to take his time.

Even as he tried to calm down, his hands were rough when he parted her trembling thighs. She cried out and he soothed her with a kiss to the soft skin right above her navel. Then he pulled back and just looked at her for long seconds. "You're so beautiful, Desi. So damn beautiful." He stroked a finger right down the center of her.

As he did, he noticed a small tattoo on her inner thigh that hadn't been there five months before. He spread her legs wider so that he could get a better look.

"I like this," he murmured, leaning forward so his mouth brushed against the tattoo. "It's new."

"I got it on a trip I took to San Francisco, be-fore I knew I was pregnant."

"It suits you." He nuzzled at the small tattoo, licked over it again and again. He moved on, skimming his lips over her hip bone and her abdomen as he stopped to explore each curve and freckle.

"I can't—Nic, I'm going to fall," Desi cried out, her hands clutching his shoulders.

"I won't let you." His mouth closed over her navel, and he fought to keep his tongue gentle as he probed her belly button and the soft skin of her belly. "I've got you, Desi. I promise. I've got you."

And then he was moving on, moving down, his lips skimming over the curve of her stomach, down the side of her hip. He made little forays under her hip bone, delicate touches and sharp little nips, all designed to make the fire burn hotter inside her.

And then he was there, right there, his mouth poised over her sex. She smelled delicious, like warm honey, and for long seconds he just knelt there, his cheek pressed against her as he tried to absorb her scent. He took a deep breath, then another and another, even as his thumbs stroked closer and closer to her slick, sexy folds.

With each slide of his thumb, Desi trembled more. With each press of his fingers into her hip, she took a shuddering breath. And when he moved forward, blowing one long, warm stream of air against her, she started to cry, her body spasming with even the lightest touch.

He was nearly as desperate as she was, his erection so hard he feared he might actually come in his pants like a teenager with his first girl. But this wasn't about him getting off, he reminded himself viciously. This was about giving Desi as much pleasure as her body could handle.

He wanted to savor her, wanted to push her higher than she'd ever gone before and then send her flying over the edge.

He knew he didn't have much longer, though, not with the way she was coming apart in his hands, her body so sensitive and responsive it humbled him even as it made him sweat.

"You're unbelievable," he muttered as he delivered one long, lingering lick along her sex. "So

sexy, so gorgeously responsive, I could just—"
He stopped talking as Desi screamed, her hands
grabbing his hair. He kissed her a second time,
then again and again, lingering each time on her
most sensitive spot.

And then his name fell from her lips like a
prayer as she hurtled over the edge of ecstasy.
He held her while she came, stoking the flames
higher and higher until she screamed silently,
her hands holding him as if he was a lifeline.
And when her body came back to earth, he held
her still and murmured sweet nonsense words
as he pressed gentle kisses to every part of her
he could reach.

When she was lucid again—when she'd
stopped trembling and her eyes grew a little
more focused, a little less dazed—she sank to
the ground beside him and started to unbuckle
his belt. Though it cost him, he stopped her with
a gentle hand over hers.

"Don't you want…?" She looked confused,
and maybe even a little hurt, which was the last
thing he was going for.

"Believe me, I want," he told her, pulling her

into his lap and cuddling her against him. "But not now, when we still have so many things unsettled between us."

"I don't understand. I thought you wanted me. I thought—" She broke off, looking away.

"Don't do that, baby. Talk to me." Gently, he turned her face back to his. "What did you think?"

"I don't know, I just…I made the no-sex rule, but I thought that was more for you than for me. And now I'm the one taking advantage of you, and—"

He laughed. He couldn't help it. "Oh, honey, you can take advantage of me anytime you want."

She pouted up at him. "I'm trying to be serious here."

"I'm being serious. Believe me. Anytime you want." He lowered his mouth to hers, slow and lingering. But as he started slipping under her spell, he heard the beat of a helicopter's propeller closing in on the building.

He pulled away reluctantly and dropped one final kiss on her forehead before gently setting her on the floor next to him. "I have to go, baby. That's my ride."

"Your ride?" She looked confused.

"The helicopter that's about to land on the roof? It's for me."

Her mouth fell open and she stared at him out of huge, shocked eyes. "I didn't think you were serious about that."

"Are you kidding me? If you think I'm going to spend five hours in traffic every day when I could be spending them with you and the baby, you are sorely mistaken."

After giving her one more kiss—he couldn't resist—he climbed to his feet. Which was no easy task considering the pain he was in after spending the night on that ridiculous sofa of Desi's.

If he didn't know any better, he would think Desi had bought the thing for the sole purpose of making him as uncomfortable as possible. Except it wasn't as if furniture stores just had these things lying around. No way could she have gotten it there on such short notice. Which meant, unbelievably, that she actually liked the thing.

"I'll be home around seven," he told her after hustling into the bathroom and grabbing his shirt off the back of the door. He buttoned it up as he slipped his feet into his dress shoes, then grabbed his briefcase and headed for the door.

He changed course at the last second, detouring to the kitchen to drop another quick kiss on Desi's lips. "If I'm going to be late, I'll text you."

"I actually have a gala to cover tonight, so I won't be here when you get back."

"A gala? Where?"

"SeaWorld. It's for Save Our Oceans—a lot of Hollywood types are supposed to be there as well as the business elite."

"Save Our Oceans—that's a good cause." He raised a brow. "Want a date?"

"A date? You mean, you really want to come?"

"Well, the last gala we attended ended pretty well, I think. So, yes. I do want to go."

She laughed. "I'm not going to have sex with you on the balcony at SeaWorld."

"A guy can dream." He pulled open the front door. "I'll send the helicopter for you and we can meet up at the gala. Sound good?"

"Yeah, I guess."

He didn't like the uncertainty in her voice. "What's wrong?"

"Nothing, it's just… I've never been in a helicopter before."

"Oh, right. Would you rather drive? I can send a car for you—"

"I'm a big girl, Nic. I am more than capable of driving myself to San Diego. That's how I met you, after all."

"I've never once doubted your capabilities. I just thought I'd have a car bring you down, we could spend the night at my place and in the morning I'll fly with you back to LA. The first time you ride in a helicopter shouldn't be by yourself. There's no fun in that."

"But what about you? You're working in San Diego tomorrow, aren't you?"

"Yeah, but the helicopter has to fly back to San Diego anyway. I'll catch a ride."

She rolled her eyes. "You'll catch a ride?"

"Okay, fine, I'll make them give me a ride." He glanced down as his phone beeped with a text. The pilot telling him they were waiting for him—as if he hadn't heard the noise of the approach. "I've got to go," he told her, "before all your neighbors revolt. Does the plan sound good to you?"

"Yes, the plan works, Mr. CEO."

"I think you've got me confused with my brother. I'm CCO. It's a very different thing."

He ducked out before she decided to throw something at him, and as he closed the door behind him, he couldn't help thinking that Desi was right. It did sound good. And so did everything else about their arrangement at the moment. Well, everything except that damn couch.

Thirteen

He'd sent a limo for her. An actual limousine, long and black with tinted windows and a driver in a full suit. And not one of those rental limousines, either—no, this limo belonged to Bijoux, and was at the disposal of the Durand brothers only. She knew that because she'd asked the driver, who had been more than happy to wax poetic about his employers.

Of course he had. Everyone *loved* Marc and Nic Durand. Everyone except her, she assured herself as she uneasily settled into the plush leather seats. She was woman enough to admit how wrong about them she'd been when she'd taken the word of a source who was more disgruntled employee than whistle-blower. She was even woman enough to admit that she liked Nic—he was pretty impossible *not* to like, after all, considering how kind and charming and supportive he was being.

But that didn't mean that she loved him. And it certainly didn't mean that she was on her way to falling *in love* with him. She barely knew the man after all.

And if that wasn't strictly true—if she knew his favorite color and how he liked to walk barefoot on the beach at midnight and that he gave huge amounts of his money away to those less fortunate and that he believed in standing up even when no one else would and that he liked his coffee with the teeniest drop of cream in it— well, that *really* wasn't *that* much to know about a person, was it? It certainly wasn't enough to make her fall in love with him when she had sworn she would never do that. With anyone. Ever.

Nic Durand could be as charming as he wanted to be, could do a million wonderful things for her and their child, and it still wouldn't matter, Desi assured herself. There was no way she would let any of that sway her from her course, no way she would let herself soften, let herself forget. No way she would let herself depend on him. Because that didn't work for her—it never had. Never would. The moment she started to believe someone cared about her, that the person wouldn't leave her—boom. That's exactly what happened.

So, no. There would be no falling for Nic, she told herself again as the limo made its way through the streets of LA before turning onto the freeway. Yes, he was living with her. Yes, they were incredibly sexually compatible, and yes, she was having his baby—but that was all there was. It was enough. More than enough. Trying for anything else would only end with one—or both—of them getting hurt.

The thought depressed her so much that she closed her eyes and willed herself not to think about it anymore. Nic had been living with her for only twenty-four hours, had been back in her life for only one week, yet the idea of him walking out of her life one day soon bothered her more than she would ever be comfortable with.

It had been a crazy day, and it wasn't long before the motion of the car had her drifting off to sleep. She'd planned on only dozing—wanting to be alert enough to answer if Nic texted her—but the next thing she knew, they were pulling into the massive SeaWorld parking lot. She reached for her phone and the directions she'd downloaded earlier on how to get to the pavilion, but the driver seemed to know exactly where he was going as he wound his way to the private entrance.

When they arrived, she thanked the driver profusely and tried to tip him, but of course he wouldn't take her money. Desi shook her head ruefully as she climbed out of the car. Having Nic around to take care of her was going to ruin her if she wasn't careful.

A glance at her phone showed she hadn't missed any texts from Nic, but then again, she'd made it to San Diego earlier than expected. She set her phone to recorder mode—which was one of the ways she kept track of who was talking to whom and what they were wearing while they were doing it—then followed the pathway up to the pavilion's main door.

Once she was checked in, she walked through the venue, scoping it out. She'd never been to a charity ball here before, and as she walked in the door, she was charmed to see the huge aquariums that surrounded the room on all sides. The decor was very much "under the sea," which was to be expected, considering the charity benefiting from the night's gala. The aquariums blended in beautifully.

She took quiet note of who was already there—not a lot of people yet whom her readers would be interested in—then made her way to the aquariums. She wanted to see the fish. She could imagine the beginning of her piece starting with the fish and expanding to the oceans and then the purpose of the gala. The society reporter before her used to focus exclusively on the glitterati, but Desi had gotten in the habit of giving her readers a little more of the atmosphere and charity angle before launching into the who's who.

So far her readers seemed to like it. Or, at least, they hadn't complained about it, so she'd take a win where she could get it.

Especially after her debacle with the Bijoux article. Her cheeks heated as she once again thought of how badly she'd messed up that whole thing. She'd spent much of last week going over her notes, trying to see where she'd gone wrong in vetting the source, but everything had checked out. Everything had seemed fine…right up until it had all fallen apart.

She still didn't understand how she had made such a terrible mistake.

Malcolm told her it was because her nose wasn't developed yet—he was always going on about how all the great investigative reporters had a nose for a story…and a nose for the truth. When she was little, before her mother had died and her father had bugged out for parts unknown, her dad used to say the same thing. But he'd told her she had that nose. That she was going to be a great reporter.

And though he'd disappointed her in a lot of different ways through the years, she'd never

doubted him when it came to that. Probably because she hadn't wanted to doubt him. Hadn't
wanted to acknowledge that the one tenuous
thing that held them together was nothing but
a lie.

As she stood staring at a particularly beautifully arranged aquarium—filled with orange
clownfish and yellow-and-blue angelfish swimming amid bright pink, yellow-and-blue sea
anemones—she was hit with the most awful
thought yet. What if she didn't really want to be
a reporter? What if she'd done all this—busted
her butt at the top journalism school in the na-
tion, worked her heart out to land the worst job
at one of the most prestigious papers in the coun-
try—not because she actually wanted to be a
journalist, but because she'd been so desperate
to get her father's attention, to make him love
her, that she'd made herself into a person she
thought he would want?

It hadn't worked. Not that it was exactly a surprise—from the moment her mother had died,
Desi had ceased to exist for her father. Then
again, everything had ceased to exist except his

job. He'd shuffled her from relative to relative, exhausting their hospitality while he chased stories overseas.

And where had that gotten them? He was dead and she was in the middle of this ballroom, taking notes about rich people and wondering if maybe her whole life up until this point had been a lie. Not exactly a stellar year for either of them, if she did say so herself.

Her soul-searching was cut off when a familiar male voice asked, "Sparkling water?"

She turned to see Nic, a glass of champagne in one hand and a glass of sparkling water in the other. He was dressed in a different tuxedo from the one he'd been wearing the night she met him, but he still looked absolutely gorgeous. Absolutely devastating. Or maybe it was just that she was devastated. She couldn't tell. All she knew was she wanted nothing more than to throw herself into his arms, burrow into his chest and pretend that everything was going to be okay.

"You look thirsty," he told her, holding out one of the glasses with a quirk of his eyebrow.

And because she knew he would take her mind

off everything that was whirling in her brain—and because she knew a perfect setup when she saw one—she took the glass from him. Then she looked over the rim and delivered her line. "Funny, I was just about to say the same thing about you."

"Were you?" he asked with the crooked grin she had come to love. "Well, you wouldn't be wrong."

She went off script then, tapping his glass. "You should probably drink up, then."

"Oh, I intend to. In fact—" He paused suddenly, his eyes darkening to the mossy green shade she loved the most. "What's wrong?"

"Nothing at all," she lied. "Why?"

"Something is," he told her as he searched her face. He was frowning now, all levity replaced by concern.

How could he tell? she wondered a little wildly, even as she calmly met his gaze. She'd learned a long time ago to keep her emotions tucked deep inside, so deep that sometimes even she forgot they were there. So how did he know?

"I can see it," he said, and for one crazy moment she thought he had read her mind. But then she realized he was reacting to her denial…and the upset she obviously wasn't as good at hiding as she'd thought she was.

"Here." He cupped her cheek in his hand, rubbed his thumb gently over the skin just beyond the curve of her mouth. "Your dimple's gone. That only happens when you're upset."

No one had ever seen that before—not even her. She'd gone through most of her adult life thinking she was one of the very few people who didn't have a tell, thinking she had hidden herself deeply enough that there was nothing for anyone to see.

And then Nic had come along and blown that idea right out of the water when they'd barely known each other a week. How did he do it? How did he see her when she couldn't even see herself?

"Desi?" he urged, stepping closer. "What's wrong?"

"Nothing—"

"Don't do that. Don't pretend with me."

"I'm not. I swear." And to her astonishment,

she wasn't. Because right then, in that moment, standing in his arms, she *was* okay. More okay than she'd been in a very long time. "It's just been a crazy day. But I'm good now."

She could tell from the look in his eyes that he understood what she hadn't been able to say—that being with him had made her okay—but he didn't push it. He didn't say anything at all. Instead, he dropped his glass of champagne on the tray of a passing waiter and pulled her into his arms.

"Is this the part where you ask me to dance?" she teased, more than ready to clear her head of painful thoughts.

"Actually, this is the part where I whisk you outside and ravish you." But contrary to his words, he swept her onto the almost empty dance floor, spinning her around to the beat of some old-time song she recognized but couldn't name.

"I thought I told you earlier that we weren't making love on the balcony this time."

He laughed, bending his head to drop a soft, sweet, *sexy* kiss on her shoulder. "Yes, but I checked. No balcony."

She laughed then, too—she couldn't help it. No matter how awful her mood was, Nic always found a way to make things better.

"So I'll take that as a yes?" he asked blithely.

"Take it as a maybe," she answered.

He quirked a brow. "*Maybe's* not *no*."

"No, it isn't." She held on while he twirled them around. "But it's not yes, ei—" She broke off midsentence, gasping and clinging to him as he suddenly lifted her up and spun her around.

"Let go," he said as he gently moved her away from his body. And though it went against every instinct she had, Desi did what he said for once. And then laughed her head off as he spun her all the way out before reeling her back in with a quick snap of his wrist.

She felt it happen right then—in the middle of the dance floor at a fancy gala that he belonged at and she certainly didn't. Desi felt herself slide headfirst into love with Nic Durand.

She spent the evening breaking all the rules. Instead of blending into the background and observing the wealthy and sometimes famous, she allowed herself to be introduced to them. To be drawn into conversations with them. Then again, it wasn't as if she had a choice.

Being Nic Durand's date meant being surrounded by people all the time. She wasn't the only one who loved him, after all. He might be new to Southern California's high society, but Nic had the kind of personality people gravitated to—and the billions of dollars at his disposal only added to his appeal. But even without the money, he was one of those guys everyone wanted to be friends with. Larger than life, funny as hell, handsome as all get out—and nice to boot. What was there not to love? God knew, she'd tried and look where it had gotten her.

Still, she couldn't quite believe that she was in the thick of things—wasn't sure that she wanted to be, if she was honest. When she'd agreed to taking him as her date, she'd kind of planned to still do the wallflower thing. Sure, she'd known he'd attract attention, but she thought that would only make it easier for her to blend in to the crowds.

But Nic wasn't okay with her blending in to the

background. Actually, he wasn't okay with her being more than two feet from him all night. Not in a creepy, possessive kind of way that would have made her champ at the bit—and probably deck him before the night was over—but in the concerned, solicitous way that said he was looking out for her. And that he was proud to have her by his side.

And so she found herself making miles of mental notes about who was doing what with whom—and what they were wearing while they were doing it. Twice, she slipped away to ostensibly use the bathroom only to spend the time hiding in a corner and talking into her recorder as fast as she could.

Not that she was talking to these people under false pretenses—everyone Nic introduced her to was told she worked for the *Los Angeles Times* and was covering the party for their society pages. But the thing was, no one seemed to care. At least that she could tell, no one acted any differently toward her at all.

At least until she met Marc Durand.

From the moment she locked eyes with Nic's

brother, she knew she was in trouble. And she couldn't even say that she didn't deserve it, because she totally did. He was the CEO of Bijoux, the man she had almost accused in print of lying, cheating, stealing and helping to fund the most egregious human rights violations. Was it any wonder he was looking at her as if he wanted to take her apart tiny piece by tiny piece? And then feed those tiny pieces to one of the sharks swimming in the tanks just beyond the pavilion?

Marc saw her and she saw Marc before Nic had a clue that anything was amiss. She tried to slip away before the eldest Durand could make a scene, but the moment she moved an inch farther away than Nic deemed acceptable, he turned to her with a frown. "Everything okay?" he asked.

She, who always had a snappy comeback, had no idea what she was supposed to say to that. And so she just shook her head, letting her eyes find Marc and his date, as they were trying to extricate themselves from the clutches of San Diego's mayor.

Nic followed her gaze, and sudden understanding flashed across his face. Then he pulled her in close, bending his head to whisper in her ear, "Everything's fine. Don't worry."

Don't worry? Easy for him to say.

He flashed Marc a grin, but Nic's older brother continued to glare at her. Which was fine, she told herself as she braced for the impending storm. She owed the man a serious apology— now was as good a time as any to get it over with. She just wished it didn't have to be in front of all these people. The humiliation of making the mistake was bad enough, but having all these people witness the fallout—people she had to work around regularly—was more than a little daunting.

Nic must not have figured that out, though, because after excusing them from a group of movie execs, he put a hand on her lower back and propelled her straight toward the center of the ballroom. Straight toward Marc.

"Hey, bro," Nic said when they reached the other couple. He clapped Marc on the back before turning to Marc's date, a gorgeous redhead with kind eyes and stunning bone structure.

"Isa, you look gorgeous tonight as always." Nic leaned down to kiss her cheek.

"I do what I can," she responded, hugging him warmly. "Keeping up with the Durand brothers isn't always easy."

"I think you've got that backward," Nic told her with a laugh. "You've certainly kept Marc on his toes through the years."

"Yeah, well, someone had to." She cast a teasing glance at the man in question, then slipped her hand into his and squeezed.

"Isn't that the truth?" He kept his hand on Desi's back as he turned to her. "Desi, this is my future sister-in-law, Isa. Isa, this is Desi." He said her name with a kind of reverence it didn't deserve, his voice soft and warm and open as he pulled her even closer into his side. It was the first clue she had—or, at least, the first one she paid attention to—that said his feelings might be as strong as hers. Panic raced through her at the thought, mingled with the discomfort she already felt upon meeting Marc. For a moment all she wanted was to find a place to hide.

But that wasn't fair—to Nic or to Marc and

Isa. Desi had screwed up royally and it was time to finish paying the piper. Which was why, when Nic turned to introduce her to his brother, she made sure to meet Marc's eyes, though it was the last thing she wanted to do. He was as handsome as his brother, but in a much colder, more stand-offish way. How did Isa avoid getting frostbite? Desi wondered as she held her hand out to him.

"It's nice to finally put a face with the name," Marc said, his blue eyes coolly assessing her as he shook her hand. "Nic's been talking about his Desi for months."

The words should have warmed her—God knew, she'd spent much of the past five months thinking about Nic, too—but there was something in the way Marc said them that made the words sound like a condemnation instead of a simple observation.

Then again, in his mind, she'd seduced his brother, gotten pregnant, then disappeared only to write an exposé full of lies about his company. The surprise wasn't that he was insulting to her. The surprise was that he was speaking to her at all.

With that thought in mind, she took a deep breath and willed herself not to screw up what she was going to say next. Which was probably easier said than done, considering how nervous she was. And how badly she'd already messed up.

"Actually, I'm really glad we're getting this chance to meet," she told him.

"Are you, now?" He lifted a brow—it was obviously a family talent, one designed to make these two men even more devastatingly attractive. And infinitely more intimidating. "And why's that?"

His tone was polite, insouciant even, but—unlike his brother—he had a tell. It was a small one, but the way his lips tightened just a little when he looked at her told her how angry he was. Which was…fair enough.

"I want to apologize for all the trouble my article caused you," she told him. Beside her, she felt Nic stiffen, then move as if he wanted to say something. Without breaking eye contact with Marc, she put a restraining hand on Nic's hip, telling him without words that she was a big girl and needed to take care of this herself.

He didn't relax at all, but at least he didn't butt in, so she counted it as a win.

"I know that's not enough," she continued, keeping her voice steady despite Marc's laser-like gaze. "Just like I know how much damage it would have done if that article had actually gone to print. I made a lot of mistakes when I was writing that article—including avoiding speaking with Nic early on because of what had happened between us—and I'm really sorry for what I put you both through."

"It's fine, Desi." Nic wrapped a protective arm around her shoulder. "Marc understands." This last was accompanied by a hard look at his brother, one that basically told Marc he'd better accept her apology or there would be hell to pay later.

She hated so much that she was a point of contention between the two brothers. They were close—she'd read that while she'd been researching her article and now, seeing them together, she knew it was true. And the fact that they were bristling at each other right now, because of her, made her a little sick.

"On the plus side," Isa said, trying to break the very obvious tension, "if you hadn't written that article, Marc and I probably wouldn't be together now. And neither would you and Nic. So, that's two good things that came out of it, right?"

"Absolutely," Nic said, and from the look on his face he actually meant it. Which seemed crazy to her after everything she'd put him through. But when he'd said clean slate, he'd really meant it. Which—again—made him a much better person than she'd ever imagined.

"That is a good point," Marc said, and he sounded friendlier than he had just a few moments before. But the tell was still there, the tightening of his lips, even when he was smiling, and she knew things weren't nearly as over as Nic wanted them to be.

Fourteen

It took only two hours for the situation to come to a head. In that time, she'd danced with Nic, recorded copious notes and even managed to make the rounds of the aquariums to see the ones she'd missed. She'd also let Nic talk her into bidding on a homemade wooden cradle for the baby, donated to the silent auction by a San Diego artisan.

It would fit really well in Nic's house, a traitorous little voice in the back of her head said. Not that she was seriously thinking of moving in with him or anything. Because she wasn't. Not yet and probably not ever. But the cradle was pretty and she would love to put her baby in it, so who cared where it went as long as it kept their son safe and happy.

"Would you like more water?" Nic asked as they finished a dance and he escorted her off the dance floor.

"Actually, I was hoping to cut in," Marc said smoothly as he appeared from nowhere. "May I have this dance?" he asked her.

She knew she should say no, knew she should make some kind of excuse and get out of it. But there was a predatory light in his eyes that told her escape wouldn't be possible—not unless she wanted to cause more trouble between Nic and Marc, which was the absolute last thing she wanted.

Besides, she would have to deal with him some time—he was her baby's uncle, after all. She might as well hear him out, let him say everything he wanted to say to her right now, and then maybe they'd be able to move past it. If she was lucky.

"I was just going to get her some water, actually—" Nic started.

"I'd love to dance," she told Marc. Then she stood on her tiptoes to give Nic a quick kiss on the cheek. "The baby and I are perfectly hydrated. So stop worrying and dance with Isa."

Then she turned to Marc and let him sweep her onto the dance floor.

He was a surprisingly good dancer. He didn't have Nic's finesse, but then again, who did? And it wasn't as if he was trying to finesse her anyway. In fact, when she glanced up at him, it looked more as though he was trying to figure her out.

It was on their second turn around the floor that she said, "Let's just get it out of the way, okay?"

He glanced down at her, brows lifted in surprise. "I'm beginning to see what Nic likes about you."

"No, you aren't. You don't want your brother anywhere near me."

"Touché." He inclined his head. "Unfortunately, Nic doesn't share my sentiments. And since you're currently carrying the first heir to Bijoux, that isn't an option anyway."

"If that's the case, then what do you want?"

"And here I was just about to ask you that question." His eyes were hard.

"I don't want anything—"

"Everybody wants something, Desi. It's the nature of the beast. And I'd rather know your endgame now than find out about it the hard way, after you destroy my brother."

"That's not going to happen."

"You're damn right it isn't going to happen, because I'm not going to let it happen. So tell me what you're after and I'll make sure you get it, in exchange for—"

"In exchange for what?" Nic asked from where he was suddenly standing between them. "What do you think you're doing, Marc?" He kept his voice down and his body language relaxed so as not to draw attention to them, but his gaze was fierce and furious. So fierce and furious that she didn't know how his brother even managed to look him in the eye.

Marc did, though, and he was easily as livid as Nic. "I'm the one who should be asking you that question, shouldn't I? This woman nearly destroyed us and now you're playing house with her? I get that she's having your baby, but you're a lot stupider than I gave you credit for if you can't figure out that even that was a setup. I don't know what her endgame is yet, but you can't be so blinded by the sex that you don't know that there is one."

Nic's hands clenched into fists as he gave up any pretense of being relaxed. "You're going to want to shut up and back off, man."

"Nic, it's fine." She tried to get his attention. "Marc's just trying to protect you."

"Yeah, well, he's doing a lousy job of it," Nic told her as he moved to put his body between her and Marc.

"Or what? You'll punch me in the middle of a charity gala?" Marc challenged him. "Go ahead. That'd be great PR for Bijoux, huh? Or has a week with her made you forget everything we've worked so hard for?"

"I think you're the one who's forgotten—"

"Stop it, Nic!" she said, grabbing his arm. She would not be the cause of them having a fight in the middle of SeaWorld, for God's sake.

"Okay, that's enough, you two." Isa stepped in then, too, grabbing Marc's arm and pulling him back a few steps. "Tomorrow in the office is soon enough to talk about this. For now—" she shot Marc a look that told him she had had more than enough "—you can take me home."

"We're not done here," Nic told her.

"Yes, you are. We all are." The look Isa gave him was as pissed off as it was understanding. "Your brother needs a time-out."

"I'm not five," Marc told her.

"Then stop acting like you are," she answered sweetly as she pulled and prodded him until he gave in.

"We're going to talk tomorrow," he told Nic before turning away.

"Damn straight we are. And it'll be your turn to apologize to Desi."

"That's not necessary, Nic," she said as Marc and Isa walked away.

"It absolutely is. You're my—" Nic broke off, shoving a frustrated hand through his hair. "He doesn't get to talk to you like that."

There was a part of her that was desperate to

know what he'd almost said, but another part knew it was better if she didn't know. Better if she didn't make what was between them—a baby—into more than it was, no matter how she felt about him.

"He's just trying to protect you, you know."

"Are we seriously having this conversation right now?" he asked as he escorted her off the dance floor. "He insulted you. Why are you defending him?"

"Because he's your brother. And he loves you. Of course he's suspicious of me—why wouldn't he be after the trouble I caused?"

Nic looked at her broodingly. "I'm not suspicious of you."

"Because you're an idiot."

"Hey!"

"Or maybe just the best person on the planet," she continued as if he hadn't interrupted her. "I haven't decided yet."

"Well, after we get back to the house, maybe I can find a way to help you make up your mind." His voice dropped several notches.

She gave him her best sultry look. "Maybe you

can." But as she let him lead her out to the parking lot—and the limo that was magically sitting at the curb waiting for them—she couldn't forget Marc's words.

Any more than she could forget the look on his face when Nic had taken her side against his.

She couldn't do that. She couldn't be the one who divided the two of them. Couldn't be the one who broke up the most important relationship in Nic's life. She'd been alone. She knew how that felt, knew what it did to you deep inside. She wouldn't wish that on anyone, let alone Nic. Wonderful, fun, exciting, beautiful, kind Nic.

But she couldn't say that to him. How could she when he was holding her and touching her and looking at her as if she'd hung the moon?

There was a part of her that wanted to wallow in it, that wanted to wrap his affection around herself and snuggle in for as long as it lasted.

What kind of person would that make her, though? It would end—of course it would end, because it always ended—and then where would he be? All alone. She couldn't do that to him. She wouldn't do that to him.

But that didn't mean she had to walk away yet. She could have this night, could have these last stolen moments with him before she had to give him up. It wasn't enough—wasn't close to being enough—but it was what she had. And she would make the best of it.

They didn't talk much during the ride. Instead, they sat close together in the back of the limo, hands touching, legs brushing. By the time the driver pulled the limo to a stop at the top of Nic's long driveway, Desi was practically vibrating with desire. With need. With a desperation that came as much from Nic himself as from knowing this would be their last time together.

The moment the front door closed behind them, Nic was on her. He whirled her around, pressed her back against the wall and then slammed his mouth down on hers. And then they were kissing, kissing, kissing, their mouths and tongues and bodies tangling together. She didn't know where she left off and he began.

It was a powerful thought, a humbling one, and it nearly broke her. How could it not when she imagined how it could have been between them. How it should have been.

His hands slid up her legs, fumbled with her underwear. But she knew if she let him touch her it would be all over. She would be lost in the maelstrom of pleasure he brought her every time he touched her.

And she wanted that—her body was scream- ing for it—but she wanted to pleasure him more. She wanted to take him as high as he took her and then watch him shatter with the ecstasy coursing through him.

Which was why she pushed him away.

"Desi?" He sounded confused and more than a little pleasure drugged. "What's wrong? Are you okay?"

She didn't answer him. Instead she put her hands on his shoulders and pushed, turning him—turning them—until he was the one with his back against the wall.

Once she had him where she wanted him, though, she took her time. If this was all she would have with him, she wanted to go slow, wanted it to last. Wanted it to be perfect.

She pulled his shirt from his pants, slowly worked the diamond studs through his button-holes. Ran her hands over his smooth, hard chest and reveled in his groans, in the soft, sexy pleas falling from his lips as she undressed him completely.

And then she was on her knees in front of him, kissing and licking and stroking as he called out her name. The sound burrowed inside her, filled her up, filled her to bursting and her heart was so wide-open that she felt it break in two even as he fell apart around her.

Fifteen

Nic woke alone.

Again.

At first he couldn't believe that she was really gone—how could he after the night they'd had? She'd made love to him as if he was her everything, as if he was the only thing, and he'd tried to make love to her the same way. Tried to tell her with his actions what she wouldn't yet believe if he told her in words—that he was in love with her. That he wanted to spend the rest of his life making her, and the baby, as happy as she made him.

Telling himself that she was up before the

alarm only so she could pack, he pulled on a pair of sweats and headed toward the kitchen to see if maybe she was making a cup of tea for herself. Or breakfast. Or—

Except the kitchen was empty. As was the rest of the house—he knew because, like an idiot, he checked every single room. She was in none of them. And he didn't know why.

She hadn't seemed angry at Marc last night. He'd been furious at his brother—was still furious—but she'd seemed strangely understanding. Had even urged Nic to get over his anger and talk to Marc about what he'd said, even though it was the last thing Nic wanted to do.

So why was she gone? Had he upset her somehow? Had he been too rough with his lovemaking? Had he hurt her? Just the thought made him sick to his stomach, and he headed back to his room to grab his phone and call her.

But when he picked it up, he saw that she had beaten him to the punch. There was a series of text messages from her that told him everything he needed to know.

I'm sorry, Nic. This isn't working. I thought I could do this, but I can't. I still plan to have the baby, and of course, you can have as large or small a part in his life as you would like. But the whole being-in-a-relationship, living-together thing…it just isn't for me. I'll have your stuff delivered to your office this week. My only request is that you don't contact me until I contact you. And I will, I promise. Just not for a little while. Thank you for everything.

Don't contact me.
Thank you for everything.
Don't contact me.
Thank you for everything.

He read the message over a dozen times. Two dozen times. Until he had it memorized so well that he didn't even need to look at it anymore and still it played in his head.

This isn't working.
Don't contact me.
Thank you for everything.

Shocked and devastated—more devastated than he had any right to be considering how little time he'd known her—he sank down onto the edge of the bed with his head in his hands. And tried to figure out what the hell had happened. What he'd done wrong. How he'd spooked her.

He was a savvy businessman and an even savvier student of human nature—he had to be to do the job he did. And yet, this time, he had nothing. Yes, Marc had attacked her at the gala, but she was the one who had stopped Nic from defending her. She was the one who had defended Marc, for God's sake. And even after that, she hadn't seemed to hold it against Nic. Instead, she'd come home with him. She'd made love to him, had let him make love to her. And it had been everything their first night together had been, only more. Because this time they'd known it meant something.

Or at least, he'd *thought* it had meant something. Now, sitting here in an empty bed that still smelled of her, he wasn't sure it had meant anything at all.

Suddenly, he wasn't sure of anything when it came to Desi and him and the relationship he'd been trying so hard to build with her. For the baby's sake…and for his.

Because he loved this woman, loved her more than he'd ever loved anyone. And though a lot of people would say it was ridiculous to fall in love with someone so quickly, he knew that wasn't the case. Because he hadn't fallen in love with Desi over the past few days as they'd tried to figure out what to do with the baby.

He'd fallen in love with her that night, nineteen weeks ago, when he'd brought her home and made love to her as if his life depended on it. Because, it turned out, it did. It really did. The life he wanted, the life he was so desperate for—with her and him and their baby—did depend on it.

And he would have sworn she felt it, too. If not that first night, then certainly last night, when they'd made love again and again and again. When he'd whispered in her ear and kissed her rounded stomach and nearly cried with how right it had all felt. When he'd held her in his arms and talked about anything and everything, including their baby and the future that they shared.

Damn it, he couldn't have been that wrong. He couldn't have imagined the look on her face or the love in her voice or the aching tenderness of her touch. He couldn't have imagined all of that.

Which meant she hadn't answered all of his questions after all. Because the one thing she was missing, the one answer she hadn't given him, was why.

And as he sat there, smartphone clutched in his hand and his heart on the floor, he knew it was the only answer that mattered.

He got to her apartment—to their apartment—before she did.

As he bounded down the stairs from the roof, he prayed he wasn't too late. That she would talk to him, listen to him and give him a chance to somehow fix whatever had gone so terribly wrong.

He hit the apartment at a dead run, spent a good five minutes knocking on the door—and listening for sounds within—as he pleaded with her to let him in before it occurred to him that a helicopter was a lot faster than a car and that Desi hadn't even made it home yet.

Once that realization dawned, he'd stood there for long seconds trying to decide between respecting her wishes and waiting outside or going in and having the element of surprise on his side. It wasn't much of a debate—he needed every bit of help he could get.

He let himself into the apartment they'd managed to share successfully for only a short while. Because he couldn't just sit—especially not on Desi's hideously ugly and uncomfortable couch—he paced the apartment while he waited, going over the arguments he'd formulated in his head on the helicopter ride up. As he stood in her apartment, watching the sun rise over the City of Angels, he couldn't help thinking that none of the arguments were good enough.

He was desperately afraid that nothing was, that there would be no way to convince her that he wanted her, that he needed her. That he loved her.

He was still angsting over it, still trying to

decide the best way to make his case, when the front door opened. And then she was there, in the foyer, staring at him with wide and exhausted eyes.

He stared back. He could do nothing else.

They stood like that for long seconds, staring at each other, a million unspoken words and thoughts and feelings arcing between them like a live wire.

And then she moved, breaking the connection between them as she dropped her overnight bag on the floor at her feet. "What are you doing here?" she asked.

"I came for you." It wasn't what he'd practiced, wasn't what he'd planned to say at all. But it was real and it was honest, which was all he had to give since she'd refused everything else.

She breathed out then, a long, slow thing that seemed to take more than air. It took her bones, her muscles, her very will, too, because the next thing he knew, she was slumped on the floor, sobbing into her knees.

He was across the apartment in a moment, dropping beside her and murmuring, "No, Desi, no. Baby, please don't cry. I'm sorry. Whatever it is I did, I'm so, so sorry."

That only made her cry harder. He didn't know if it was emotional or hormonal or a little bit of both, but it broke his heart to see her in so much pain. Nearly killed him to think that he had somehow been the cause of it. When he could take it no more, he ignored her hands pushing him away and pulled her into his lap.

"Don't—"

"Shh," he told her, one hand cupping her head while the other stroked her back. "Just relax and let me take care of you."

"I don't need you to take care of me," she said even as her hands came up to curl in his shirt.

"Believe me, I am well aware of that fact." He continued to rock her anyway. "But I need to hold you right now. Please, let me hold you."

She kept crying, but she didn't protest again. She just curled into a ball on his lap and sobbed into his chest. And sobbed. And sobbed. And sobbed.

When he could take it no more, when his heart was in danger of breaking wide open under the force of her sorrow, he bent his head. Brushed soft kisses over her temples and down her cheek. And pleaded, "Desi, please, tell me what's wrong. Let me help. Please, sweetheart—"

He broke off as she stiffened in his arms, flashed back to the last time he'd called her sweetheart and what her reaction had been. "I'm sorry—"

"Stop saying that," she told him as her tears died down. "None of this is your fault. It's mine."

"It's ours," he told her. "I'm doing something that's pushing you away, and whatever it is, I'm sorry for it. But please, Desi, you have to talk to me. You can't just walk away like we're nothing. You're carrying my baby—"

"I already said you could see the baby whenever you want."

"And I appreciate that. I do. But it's not just the baby I want."

"You don't mean that."

"I do mean it."

"You can't." She struggled against his hold, climbing off his lap the second he let her go.

He was up in a second, following her across

the apartment—at least until she held up a hand and said, "Stop. Just…stop for a second, please."

"Yeah, okay." He froze in place. "Sure."

She laughed then, and somehow it was the saddest sound he'd ever heard. "Why do you have to be so perfect?" she asked.

"I'm not—"

"You are. I knew it that first night. Everything about you was so, so right for me, and it scared the hell out of me. It sent me running away from you as far and as fast as I could go. And it would have been okay. If you had just stayed gone, everything would have been all right. Instead you're here and you're breaking my heart—"

"I don't want to break your heart," he told her, crossing to her because he couldn't not touch her when he told her this. "And I don't want you to break mine. I love you. I'm in love with you, Desi, and I want to be with you. I want to marry you. Why is that so hard for you to understand?"

"Because no one ever has."

"Wanted to marry you?" He hoped not. He hated the very idea of her being close enough to another man to even entertain the idea.

"Loved me."

"That can't be true."

She bowed her head, wrapped her arms around her stomach in a move that was so obviously self-protective that it broke his heart. "It is true. No one has ever loved me. I mean, except my mother and she died when I was nine, so…it's been a while.

"My dad freaked out when she died. He couldn't handle it and he certainly couldn't handle me. He was a reporter, too. One of the best investigative journalists in the world. And the day after my mother's funeral, he parked me with my grieving grandparents and took off to find a war to cover.

"He came back a few months later, just in time to have a fight with my grandmother and take me off her hands. Not because he wanted anything to do with me, mind you, but to punish her for saying he was being a terrible dad. Two weeks later, he dumped me on his college roommate and his wife, and took off again. Six months later he showed back up because they were having their own kid and didn't want me around anymore. So he brought me to visit his sister and snuck out on her in the middle of the night.

"The night he left, I knew he was going to go. He called me sweetheart when I went up to bed. And I knew. He only ever called me sweetheart right before he left me. My aunt kept me for three months before she shipped me off to my mother's brother. And that's pretty much how it went until I graduated high school and left for college.

"And you know the worst part? At the gala last night, I realized I've done all this for him. I worked like a dog to get a degree in journalism from Columbia. I've spent two years writing ridiculous articles that I don't care about for the *Los Angeles Times*. I took the assignment on Bijoux, even knowing that I shouldn't have, and we all know how that turned out. I did it all, hoping that one day he'd be proud of me. That one day he would come back and see what I'd done and he'd tell me I'd done a good job." Her voice broke. "How pathetic is that? How ridiculous and pathetic am I?"

"You're not pathetic at all."

She snorted. "Yeah, right."

She wouldn't look at him. He wanted, so badly, to see her face, but she wouldn't lift her head. Wouldn't let him see.

Jesus. He didn't have a clue what he was supposed to say, how he could talk about this without sounding like a total douche. Sure, he'd had absentee parents—a father who cared more about screwing around with women half his age than he ever did about his family and a mother who cared more about status than she did about her husband screwing around on her—but through it all, Nic had always had a home. He always knew where he was going to be sleeping and what his routine would be like and whom he would see at school. And he'd always, always, had Marc. His brother might be a busybody with trust issues a mile wide, but he was a great big brother. He'd never once been anywhere but in Nic's corner.

Who had been in Desi's corner? he wondered as she put on the kettle for tea. Who'd had her back when she'd needed it most? The idea that there had been no one, that the woman he loved had essentially been on her own at the age of nine, wounded him on a visceral level.

"That's why you kept the baby. So you'd have someone to love you."

"Maybe." She shrugged as she put a tea bag in a cup. "I thought about having an abortion but I just…couldn't. And I could never give him up for adoption. I'd go crazy wondering if he was okay, if he was with someone who loved him or if he was just—" Her voice broke, but she swallowed. Tried again. "Or if he was just being tolerated. I can't stand the idea of him being any-where he isn't loved."

Nic did cross to her then, did pull her into his arms and let his hands rest on her tummy. On their baby.

"That will never happen to him," he assured her. "We'll never *let* that happen to him. He will know every day of his life that he is loved. And so will you, if you'll trust me. If you'll let me love you. I'm not saying I won't make mistakes, as I'm pretty new to this serious-relationship thing, too. But I promise you, Desi, that if you let me, I will love you forever. I will be there when you wake up and I will be there when you fall asleep and I will be there all the times you need me in between."

"You don't know that."

"I do know it, Desi."

Another sob racked her body and she covered her mouth to silence the sound. "Don't say that," she said when she could speak again. "Don't say it if you don't mean it."

"I never say things I don't mean." He got in her face then, circled her upper arms with his hands and waited until she looked up at him. Until she looked him in the eye. "I love you," he told her. "I will love you tomorrow. I will love you next year. I will love you in twenty years if you'll let me. I will—"

She stopped him with a kiss, one that stole his breath and most of the brain cells in his head. Which was why, when she finally pulled back, all he could do was stare at her dumbly.

"You should be careful what you promise," she told him when they both finally caught their breath.

"I'm always careful with my promises," he answered. "Because I never break them."

"I know." She pressed a soft kiss to his lips. "I almost never make promises, either, because I don't believe in breaking them. But I'll make a promise to you, if you'll let me."

Let her? He nodded eagerly. Too eagerly if her muffled laugh was anything to go by. But he couldn't help it. He'd die to hear her tell him that she loved him. That she wanted him to be a part of her and the baby's lives.

"Then it's my turn to make a promise. And I promise you, Nic Durand, that I will love you for as long as I live. I will live with you in that great big house of yours by the ocean. I will laugh with you. I will raise children with you. And I will love you until I die."

Tears bloomed in his eyes, too, but when he reached for her, she held up a hand to stop him. "I'm not done yet."

She'd already told him everything he wanted to hear, so much more than he had imagined her conceding when he'd climbed in that helicopter to chase after her. But he just nodded, and waited for whatever else she had to say.

"Not only all of that, but I also promise to never, ever, *ever* write another article about you or your brother or your company as long as we both shall live."

He laughed then, because how could he not? He was getting everything he'd ever wanted, and all he had to do was fall in love with the most wonderful woman in the world. He kind of felt as if he'd cheated the system, and won. It was a beautiful feeling, one he would cherish for the rest of his life.

And as he swept her into his arms and carried her the twenty-two steps necessary to take her through the living room and into the bedroom, he did ask her for one more thing. A new couch.

He counted it as a sign that she loved him that she laughed only a little…and gave in with only a very little struggle.

* * * * *